Special thanks to
John, Barbara, and Carl

Books by M K Scott

The Talking Dog Detective Agency
Canine Cozy Mystery

A Bark in the Night

Requiem for a Rescue Dog Queen

Bark Twice for Danger

The Ghostly Howl

Dog Park Romeo

On St. Nick's Trail

The Painted Lady Inn Mysteries Series
Culinary Cozy Mystery

Murder Mansion

Drop Dead Handsome

Killer Review

Christmas Calamity

Death Pledges a Sorority

Caribbean Catastrophe

Weddings Can be Murder

The Skeleton Wore Diamonds

Death of a Honeymoon

Cakewalk to Murder

Sailors Take Warning

Late for Love

By

M K Scott

Chapter One

THE LATE MORNING sun illuminated the senior citizens below, bringing with it a touch of heat. Indian Summer was the common name for the hot weather that stretched into Autumn. For the residents of Greener Pastures Convalescent and Retirement Center, it was a bonus. Too often, they were trapped inside with the mingled scents of antiseptic cleaner and the lingering aroma of whatever was burnt in the kitchen that day. A gathering of five residents took enjoyed the warm weather.

Being bored, the senior sleuths had gathered in the courtyard for a little croquet. Marcy suggested they should take advantage of their leisure time before she made her exit from the facility, taking with her any possibilities of solving more cold cases. A mockingbird perched on the edge of a gutter broke into full-throated song, breaking Jake's concentration as he glared at the painted ball on the patchy grass.

Who invented this game anyhow? What was so great about hitting a wooden ball through wire hoops? He might be old and living in a senior home, but he was still a veteran pilot, which should count for more than a cracked leather jacket and a handful of memories.

His former war buddies, Herman, and Gus, lived at the center along with their sweeties, Lola, and Eunice. Herman and Lola had tied the knot in Vegas *and* North Carolina recently, which was a story. Feeling even more like an extraneous fifth wheel when it came to the two couples made Jake sigh.

"Come on." Eunice brandished her mallet as if she might use it to encourage Jake. "Quit stalling. None of us want to waste what time we got left watching you trying to remember how to hit a ball."

He glared at Eunice, who smirked back. Even the sharp-tongued harpy had found love, while he had not. What did that say about him? The wooden mallet made a solid thud as it connected with the ball, sending it rolling only to bounce off the wire hoop. Dagnabbit!

Before Eunice could remark on his poor shot, the glass doors leading to the residence wing opened with a distinctive groan. Marcy and Lance, her former partner, stood framed in the opening for a second before stepping into the courtyard. Despite the surgery on her shattered leg and her time spent recovering, Marcy still leaned on Lance. It probably had more to do with affection than her ability to walk, but it could be a little bit of both.

The senior sleuths didn't need to use their deductive skills to notice the budding romance between the two former partners. It was hard to believe you could work side by side with someone for years and never notice the attraction or possibly never act on it. However, he wasn't one to talk with one failed marriage and no serious relationships after that. On the good side, their appearance detracted from the tedium of the game.

"Good morning!" Marcy trilled while flashing a cheery smile.

The dark-haired detective could be counted on to bring out the best in folks. She took a seat on a nearby bench and glanced around, possibly checking if there might be an extra resident who hadn't been a part of the Senior Sleuths organization who might be eavesdropping. While residing at Greener Pastures, Lance had brought Marcy cold cases to keep her mind active and obviously, to visit. Since some of the cases were so old, she came up with the idea of enlisting help from a few select residents who could remember old street names, places long ago torn down, and knew many of the associated rumors.

Solving the cases had been the highlight of his current existence. Jake might even put it up against being an air force pilot because as a pilot, he never saw the direct results of his work and could only speculate if he'd done any good. As a Senior Sleuth, he could take pride in helping round up criminals who had gone scot-free for so many years.

Everyone abandoned their mallets to crowd around Marcy.

"How have you two been?" Gus asked in an overloud voice. Having worked in explosive ordinance, his hearing wasn't the best. It didn't help that he also refused to wear a hearing aid. He said it was something old people wore.

Lance grinned, but Marcy answered as she slipped off the straps of a backpack and pulled it onto her lap. "It's been okay. Getting to know my house again. I'm back at work, but they have me riding a desk."

Even before she left, Marcy made her feelings known about being tied to the desk. All the sleuths managed a sympathetic murmur or word.

Lola, the former showgirl with her elaborate coiffure and acrylic nails, used her walker to ease closer and sit down on the bench. She patted Marcy's hand. "Tough break. At least you have a job. I know you were worried about being forced into early retirement."

"True enough." Marcy forced a laugh, withdrew her hand from under Lola's, and placed it on the backpack in her lap. "I'm not here to whine. Frankly, I miss you guys. It seems like it has been forever since we worked on our last case, as opposed to only having been a month."

Herman, a tall, portly man, nodded his silvery head in agreement. "Feels even longer to me. Have you solved any more cold cases on your own?"

A throat clearing drew their notice to Lance. Even though the detective was a few years younger than Marcy's fifty, most people would never guess it with his thinning hair and pot belly. Still, his grin retained a touch of boyishness. "Leave it to you to cut to the chase."

His eyes landed on Herman, and he then went on to make eye contact with all the sleuths. "I think you might be interested in what Marcy has to say."

This sounded promising. "I'm listening," Jake said, not making the mistake to answer for the others. He'd learned on previous occasions the error of assuming too much.

"Me, too!" Herman echoed.

Lola and Eunice also agreed, while Gus held a hand up to his ear and asked, "What?" with an impish look.

Eunice elbowed him and didn't bother repeating the question. It was always hard to tell if he hadn't heard or was just jerking their chains.

Instead of replying, Marcy unzipped her backpack with a metallic zing, filling the silence that stretched between them. She removed some manila folders with typewritten labels and numbers. Jake's shoulders went back, and his chin went up as he recognized cold

4

case files. His day just got better. It made him feel like he should salute and report for a mission.

The files made a shushing sound as Marcy shuffled them casually as a person would a deck of cards. "You'd be surprised at the dozens of cold cases we have. At first, I thought Lance was bringing me files to solve because he felt sorry for me."

"Nope." Lance grimaced. "The budget is limited, and there are no new hires in sight. Besides, anyone who gets hired will start out on active cases. There's no *manpower*." He cleared his throat when Marcy arched her eyebrows at the last word. "I mean *people power* to deal with the cold cases. We do what we can, but usually move from one active case to the next."

"That's why we're here." Marcy spread out the folders and used them as a fan. "Sure, I missed you guys, but I could use a little help, too. Anyone interested?"

There was a chorus of *yeses* with Herman raising his hand as if still in the classroom.

Eunice, even though she was the shortest, worked her way in front of Marcy and plucked a folder at random. "I'll take this one."

Even though they were used to the woman's bossy ways, no one took it lying down.

Lola snatched the plump folder from Eunice and opened it. She blinked a couple of times to bring it into focus without any luck, and then retrieved her readers that hung on a chain around her neck. "Let's see what we have here before you go volunteering us for a case that is older than we are."

The pages whispered as they turned, as if sharing their contents. Every now and then, Lola would murmur something inaudible to herself. Her legs were crossed, and one foot would vary in its rate of swinging.

Whatever it was had to be good. Jake could barely stand it. "Out with it. What is it? A bludgeoned body? A jewelry heist?"

Lola closed the folder and waited. As a former showgirl, she knew how to pick a moment. Satisfied that she was the focus, she tapped the folder with a fuchsia-colored nail. "We have a real live mystery. It was in the papers not so long ago." She flipped the folder open, consulted the file, and addressed the group. "Two years to be exact. A young investigative journalist had the goods on some big rollers. She was supposed to be a prime witness, but then she went missing. Not only that, the evidence vanished with her." She gave the file another tap. "Makes me wonder why they gave up so easily with this one."

Lance made a lunge for the folder. "I don't think that would be a good one for you guys. It might be too dangerous."

Lola pulled the folder close to her ample chest, refusing to hand it over.

A loud harrumph came from Gus, proving his hearing might be better than most assumed. "Remember when I got trapped by that drug lord? What about when that house was almost demolished with us in it? You think it's worse than that?"

"I don't know," Lance admitted with his shoulders slumping a little. "I just don't want you to get hurt."

"No worries," Jake said to reassure the well-meaning detective. "I figure all of us must be doing something right since we made it this far. Besides, if we encounter any trouble—even a whiff of danger—we'll call you right away."

Lance sniffed, shot Jake a doubtful look, and nodded. "I guess that could work. Feel free to call, and we'll come by after work to check your progress." He checked his watch. "We have ten more minutes before we need to go."

Wrought iron chairs and a few benches sat in random spots in the courtyard. At one time, there might have been some organization to it, but various residents rearranging them made the area look like an abandoned jacks game played with outdoor furniture.

Eunice walked over to a chair and pulled it closer to Marcy. "Let's circle around and find out more about our newest case."

Even though it galled Jake to take any direction from Eunice, he did. He wanted to find out about the case, too.

Chapter Two

ASMALL DECORATIVE wrought iron table better suited for the occasional coffee cup or iced tea served as a work counter as Marcy laid out various items from the file. Several black and white photos, along with color snapshots, showed a dark-haired woman with intense eyes. In some photos, she was standing with other people.

The sleuths crowded around the table, most with their readers perched on their noses. Lola made a tsking sound and gestured to the photos. "So young. Just a baby."

Herman, Lola's new husband, hovered behind her and peered at the image. "How can you tell? Anyone under the age of fifty looks young to me."

With a flutter of paper, Marcy held up a photo. "Lyre McCovey was thirty-nine. She's considered dead, although there was no identification found on the body."

"Body?" Gus commented without asking for the soft-spoken detective to speak up. It confirmed Jake's theory that Gus could hear just fine, or maybe he had selective hearing. Plenty of people had that.

"Ah, about that…" Marcy said and hesitated. She made brief eye contact, grimaced, and examined the empty manila folder in her lap.

She was trying to protect them. For some reason, younger people always assumed their elders were porcelain dolls that would break with the slightest shock or off-color remark. It never occurred to them that the same alleged porcelain dolls had dealt with war, famine, disease, and various other calamities. You didn't live as long as he had by being some shrinking violet. "Go on. Gus, Herman, and I have been in battle. Lola worked in Vegas. As for Eunice, I'm sure..." He stopped, not wanting to talk for Eunice and possibly imagining any disasters of major proportions in Eunice's life that she'd probably orchestrated.

"As for me," Eunice held up one hand as if testifying, "I've seen things. Ugly things."

Since she had mentioned when working on a previous case that she'd worked in a furniture showroom, Jake wondered if she might be talking about crushed velvet furniture.

It seemed to satisfy Marcy, who cleared her throat. "In the court case that was supposed to happen, Lyre had information on the mob boss, Tony Delmonico."

Eunice leaned forward and asked in a shocked tone. "The Macaroni King?"

"Pasta was a side business. It was believed he used it to launder money. Lyre supposedly had proof. The Feds wanted to keep her in a safe house, but the word was she went paranoid, convinced she was being followed. Said something about she could trust no one." She arched her eyebrows and muttered. "Looks like she was right. Anyhow, shortly after her disappearance and the cancellation of the trial, a body washed up on the Louisville side of the Ohio River. A mob hit—or it was assumed to be."

While Jake never considered himself an expert on organized crime, he had watched a few movies about it. "Bullet to the back of the head?"

"No." Marcy stalled again, and then said, "There was no head, no hands, and no feet. Really nothing to go on. It was a woman's body who was over twenty-four due to the skeletal morphology. No sign of childbirth and some wear on the knees, which would indicate a job or hobby that put a lot of stress on the legs. We could only go on the skeleton since the body was bloated from its time in the water, making it unrecognizable. The medical examiner asked Lyre's sister Lorelei to come in for the ID. It's not clear if she did."

"Horrible thing," Lola concluded, pressing her hand over her heart. "Who would name their kids such artsy-fartsy names?" Perhaps feeling some embarrassment over her comment, she tacked on another. "I certainly wouldn't want any of my siblings to identify *my* corpse."

There was a murmur of agreement among the sleuths, even those who didn't have siblings. "So," Jake held up one finger. "You're saying Lyre might not be dead?"

"Not exactly." Marcy spaced out the words. "She *could* be dead. Could be buried in a shallow grave or any other of the creative ways criminals dispose of bodies. What I am saying is no one knows whose body washed ashore. Lorelei wasn't too helpful. She and her sister weren't close, which meant she didn't receive any important calls explaining she was in trouble or all-important letters starting with *if you received this, then I am dead.* She didn't even know if Lyre had tattoos. The body had a single lily tattoo at the small of the back."

"Odd," Eunice was first to react. "Most women would have picked a rose. Still, if she and her sister weren't close…" She left the statement half-finished and shrugged her shoulders. "Nothing else from the sister?"

Most folks might find Eunice's question a tad rude since it sounded like she was doubtful. Still others might get hot thinking she was calling them or whoever wrote the report a liar. Not Marcy, though. The woman could be as cool as a cucumber and besides, she knew Eunice could be a great help when she chose to be. When it came to thinking of getting away with things, Eunice was your girl. Her sharp mind, sly manner, and gumption would have served her well as a master criminal. Come to think of it, there wasn't any proof Eunice hadn't been one since she was clever enough to never mention it.

"Just a minute." Marcy opened her phone and typed, glanced at the number on the case, and typed some more. "Due to issues with missing evidence and the possibility of fire, we've started backing up our cold case information for the past five years on the cloud. If it's older than that, we're still dealing with hard copies. Okay, let me see. The officer on this case was…"

Two birds chose that moment to enter a discussion that involved a great deal of wing fluttering and screeching, drowning out what she might have said. Lance must have heard because he asked, "Lee Greer?"

"Possibly. It's L. Greer. I don't think we have more than one Greer."

Lance folded his arms as he worked his chin back and forth. "I remember him. He probably has twelve to fifteen years on me. I think he retired. He was someone who didn't suffer fools gladly. His notes should be interesting."

Here they were reminiscing about a veteran cop as opposed to reading notes. Jake shifted his weight from foot to foot and jingled the change in his pocket. He considered it a gentle way to signal his impatience. Not everyone did. Herman sent him a disapproving look, but Eunice, who was closer, nudged him with her elbow. He stopped jingling and shuffling his feet as Marcy read.

"*Called at the home of sister of the victim. She was surprised at Lyre's death, but not overly concerned. Did ask if she could retrieve parrot from sister's apartment. Weird that she remembered the parrot, but couldn't ID the clothes found on the floater.*"

"A parrot!" Gus clapped his hands together. "Maybe *he* knows the name of the killer."

While Jake had nothing against the chatty birds, he didn't think it was the secret to the case. "A neighbor of mine had an African Grey once. She told me it mimicked the lawnmower *and* a crying baby. Can you imagine that all day long?"

"Could be worse," Gus added. "What if it heard a machine gun or an air raid siren? Hearing that all day would be enough to drive a person crazy."

There was a loud throat-clearing before Herman could weigh in on what annoying noise a bird could make. Marcy grinned at all of them. "Boy, I missed you guys. Now, getting back to the case." She consulted her phone. "*Sister took the parrot. They went through the apartment inch by inch. Didn't find anything. The lack of information was curious. A journalist with her sources should have had records. Someone as paranoid as she was wouldn't trust anyone else or even the cloud. There was no laptop or desktop, no thumb drives, folders, or even a file cabinet. There was a comment in the file that the apartment was devoid of all pertinent information. Outside of the parrot, half a bottle of soda, and part of a delivery pizza in the fridge, it looked like no one lived there or someone was planning on leaving soon."*

"Not soon enough." Lola sighed heavily. "Poor gal."

"I hear you," Marcy added. "This is what we know. She was one of the best in her field. Work consumed her life, crowding out any hopes of a family. I can relate to that."

Without saying a word, Lance stepped up behind his former partner and placed a hand on her shoulder. She covered it with her own and continued speaking. "I considered trying to solve this case myself." She shook her head before speaking, "Decided there wasn't enough information. There are only a handful of articles the woman wrote hinting at corruption among the higher-ups. She pointed the finger at more than a few officials, although you'd have to read between the lines. It's not enough to accuse her of libel. You'd have to be thinking the same person is guilty to get the hints. Besides, not sure if public officials can sue for defamation. It's just part of the job."

The door opened, stopping conversation as two cotton-topped senior residents entered the courtyard. They nodded at the group and headed to the croquet set. One woman picked up a club and gave it a hearty swing as if it were a scythe and she was cutting wheat. The other woman picked up Jake's ball and moved it. Thank goodness for that. He had no desire to continue the play.

While Marcy gathered up the photos and articles, Eunice moved away from the table. She stood facing the women with her hands on her hips. "Gladys! Myrtle! What are you doing? You waltzed in and take over the croquet set without even asking?"

The woman with the mallet swung it slowly back and forth as if she'd forgotten it was in her hand or possibly to be threatening. "Get off your high horse. I know you know about the croquet tournament. Even now you're planning your strategy." She brought up the mallet to point to Lance and Marcy. "I think you're going to bring in those two kids as ringers. It won't work. They don't live here."

Everything was starting to come together. No wonder Eunice had wanted them to play croquet—a game he was certain only children played at family reunions and boring ones at that. Jake had suffered through bingo, shuffleboard, and square dancing. No way was he getting involved with croquet. His only interest was bringing justice to Lyre, who almost everyone appeared ready to shelve among the cold cases.

Chapter Three

THE GLASS EXIT doors revealed aproned center employees pushing heavy carts crowded with orange insulated meal trays. Looked like it was lunchtime. Jake knew the trays would sit in the hall for almost thirty minutes before being delivered to the residents—just another reason he enjoyed eating in the dining room, besides the basic fact that he could. Even though he'd admit it to no one, it also allowed him to catch up on center gossip.

Eunice's voice carried as she fussed with the newest arrivals, Myrtle and Gladys. "Don't bother entering. You don't stand a chance."

"We'll see about that!" declared Myrtle with both hands on her hips and a determined tilt to her chin. Rumor around the center was the woman was as big a know-it-all as Eunice. Jake wasn't sure who he'd put his money on. It would be like the clash of the titans—only the geriatric version.

Case papers gathered and stored in the file, Marcy stood, ready to leave. "Well, I just wanted to see which one would work for you. I'll get copies for you and return soon."

Lola and Herman were quick to agree while Gus kept watch on Eunice, probably afraid a fight might break out and he'd have to intercede. If the file left with Marcy, as it looked like it would, he'd be left with nothing more than Matlock reruns and possibly being herded to the courtyard for more croquet practices. "Wait!"

Marcy stopped in mid-action of stuffing the file into the back-pack. "Jake, what is it?"

The woman knew how to address folks by using their names. She would have made a good salesperson. The same skills that would have enabled her to sell a life insurance policy probably served her well to deescalate a dangerous situation, possibly extract information from an informant, or even nail down a confession, especially if she accompanied it with her current concerned look.

"I was wondering if I could copy some of those articles to read. You know my niece has a copier in her office." Jake didn't have a ton of relatives, but he did have a niece and a grandnephew in the area. It helped him decide on the center. Gus begging influenced him, too.

Every now and then, he took advantage of his connection by using his niece Katie's copier to make copies. She never asked what they were for as long as he didn't abuse the privilege with too frequent use. His niece even gave him her old laptop, which he could use to tie into the center's WIFI.

Marcy pursed her lips as if considering the matter. Technically, the case files shouldn't leave the precinct. Never mind the Senior Sleuths were solving the cases and not taking credit for doing so. All credit and responsibility fell on Marcy and Lance. If something went wrong, which it did at times, the cavalry in the form of the police showed up assuming they were just befuddled old folks in the wrong place at the wrong time. It was frustrating not to point out that their diligence and intelligence solved cold cases that had long been forgotten.

Before she could answer, Lance did. "Seems fair. You can walk us out and we'll stop by Katie's office on the way."

That sounded like a great plan. This way he could be the lead sleuth. Maybe it hadn't been anyone's intention, but lately, he felt the other sleuths had grabbed onto a case and had run with it. Jake scampered to the door to hold it open for the detectives. He held up his hand in greeting and called out to the rest of the sleuths, "See you at lunch."

About ten minutes later, Jake sat at a scarred maple dining table perusing his copies of the articles. Fortunately, he enlarged and darkened the articles for easy reading. He stacked the copies into two piles—the ones he'd read and those he hadn't.

The aroma of chicken and dumplings wafted on the air, making Jake's stomach growl. The old-fashioned meals were what the cooks did best. Not so long ago, Eunice and Gus staged a rally to protest the poor quality of the food. The penny-pinching dietitian left, along with her dismal meals. Thank goodness for that. The new dietician now and then tried something called *gastronomic creations* where she tried to make the food trendy by sticking a leaf or a flower on it. She tried to trick folks by whipping together turnips and mushrooms and calling it healthy mashed potatoes. She only did this for the dining room crowd, but she must have gotten so much feedback about it that it stopped. On the other hand, it might have been too much work, making things look like what they weren't.

Gus was the first one to join him. His friend pulled out a chair and angled his head in the direction of the articles. "Find anything out?"

It seemed like a cheap way of getting out of reading. Jake placed his hand on the already read copies and pushed them in front of Gus. "You read them and tell me."

A derisive snort greeted his pronouncement. Gus picked up the first article and held it out at arm's length and squinted. Just like the hearing aid, glasses were something for the old and something the man refused to wear. The fact they were all living in an assisted living community should have been a nod to the fact they *were* old. No forty-something man still knee-deep in the rat race ever said, "Hey, I think I'll go live in a senior center." Or at least, none he'd met. Jake blew out a breath, aware he'd recap the entire article for Gus if for no other reason than to humor the man with his refusal to accept the obvious. Of course, Eunice could come dashing in and interrupt his summary, insisting that somehow, he hadn't read it right or some other conclusion.

"Ah, where's Eunice?"

"Practicing her putting. Apparently, she's rattled Myrtle might get the jump on her as far as the croquet tournament. You know my gal. She's a touch competitive." Gus chortled and put down the article, possibly waiting for Jake to react.

Nope, it was way too easy. Most folks knew enough to get out of Eunice's way. It might do her some good to have some actual competition. Instead, Jake pointed to the article that Gus had discarded. "Looks to me like Lyre has a ton of anonymous sources."

"Hmm," Gus nodded his head, then twisted in his chair to stare at the kitchen, which made Jake wonder if he was even listening. It *had* to be selective hearing. Determined to repeat himself a tad louder, Jake started.

"I said!"

Gus grumbled. "I heard you the first time. I'm not deaf."

That prognosis was still up in the air. "What did I say then?"

"The missing woman made up a bunch of stuff."

"Did not." Partial hearing loss could be a possibility, but that could be true for Jake or most of the residents, too. He held up his index finger and shook it as he spoke. "Anonymous source doesn't equate lies."

Once he caught sight of his upraised finger, he hurriedly put it down. Geesh, he looked like every other old dude lecturing anyone who would listen about how things were different in his day, all while shaking a scolding finger. That wasn't the way he wanted to think of himself. If Gus pretended not to be old, Jake would do his best not to be a stereotype of the elderly. After all, how many of the silver set solved cold cases if you discounted all the television detectives? Precious few, and he was one of them.

Their sleuthing activities were always on the QT, so Jake leaned closer to say. "Whoever her sources were, they knew where the bodies were buried."

"Bodies? I thought there was only one!" Gus boomed in an over-loud voice, attracting the attention of a passing aide who shot them a curious look but nothing more. Sometimes, the belief that anyone over fifty was confused served them well.

"It's an expression," Jake continued in a normal tone. He'd dis-covered too much whispering attracted attention from the residents who thought they were being gossiped about and others who were just nosy. "Anyhow, turns out whatever she was told was correct. Lyre won the Livingston Award for outstanding journalism for those under the age of thirty-five. Plus, she did some television news show that won the Edward R. Murrow award for electronic media. A Pulitzer Prize was a possibility if she had finished her last investiga-tion. I heard some folks can even get it after death."

19

"After death," Gus echoed his words. "I don't see the point. Where did you come up with all this info? I doubt the woman would write it about herself. How could she work it into the article and all?"

Gus had a point. Although online, bloggers listed their credentials at the top or the bottom of the article to prove it was worth reading and not just another opinion piece or political rant. Jake ruffled through the papers to get the one he wanted, but remembered his friend wouldn't be able to read it, so he left his hand on top of the articles. "Got it from her obituary. I guess it was written up by the paper. In some ways, she was a minor celebrity and they just wouldn't let her passing go without comment."

Gus muttered something too low for Jake to hear. The man did it on purpose, just to have him ask, "What?"

"Oh?" Gus raised his eyebrows. "You didn't hear me? I said it as clear as day."

"No, you didn't." Out of the trio of battle buddies, Gus was always the jokester. No way would Jake allow him to gaslight. "Might as well say it now. We can't do much if we don't communicate."

"Communicate." Gus tilted his chair back and folded his arms. His gaze passed over Jake before arching up to the ceiling where the fan slowly turned, creating a minor breeze. Just about the time Jake was certain his friend had lost his train of thought, his chair thumped down and Gus slapped the table.

"What if Lyre is still alive? Maybe all of this is to ease the suspicions of whoever she might have had the goods on."

The thought rolled around in his mind, gathering speed. "You know, you might be right. No wonder no one's tried too hard to find her, knowing she was alive the entire time. I think you got it, Gus."

Instead of being elated about solving a crime with mere logic, Gus grimaced. "I never said I believed it. Just throwing it out there. What about the headless torso?"

Yeah, that was a problem that had no explanation. It looked like they were back to square zero. An excess of clues would be a bad deal because he didn't want to solve the case too quickly or he'd be back watching reruns and Heaven forbid, playing croquet.

Herman's tall form was easy to spot as he entered the room. Most of the time, he hovered over Lola making sure his wife's path was smooth without any bunched carpet or cracked tile. This afternoon there was another lady with them. A tall beauty who held up her head with dignity. Even though her step was sure, Jake's heart sank. It wasn't that he didn't like women, he did, but he seldom made it to a second date. The one thing he didn't know how to do was to maintain a relationship. Once people married, they inevitably try to fix up their friends.

His best option was to leave now before the introduction. He gathered up his articles and stuffed them into an oversized envelope his niece so thoughtfully provided. For whatever reason, Gus decided to snag an article and held it up as if reading it. "Give it to me. I need to leave, now."

No response. Gus's eyes moved left to right as if he were reading, which made Jake wonder if the not being able to see was a pretension or if feigning to read was the actual act. Before he could decide, Herman and crew arrived at the table, leaving no opportunity to gracefully depart.

Chapter Four

CONVERSATION PICKED UP at the other tables as Herman arrived in the dining room with a woman on each arm. Some speculated on the identity of the unknown woman. Necks craned as the residents leaned forward to get a better view. Normally, Jake didn't mind the spotlight if he'd planned the moment for his benefit. This wasn't one of those times.

Jake forced a smile, stood, and even pulled out a chair for the new arrival as good manners dictated. The woman murmured her thanks as she gracefully took her seat. A giggle sounded behind him, possibly one of the trio of women who usually sat at a nearby table. Could be they thought they had front row seats to a new romance. Instead of turning on the charm, aggravation stabbed at him since there would be no opportunity to discuss the case. The article in Gus's hand would be hard to ignore. Not good, not good at all. The senior sleuths had managed to solve four cases without letting anything slip. He tried to keep eye contact with the newest arrivals while gesturing for the article his friend held. Dinner's immediate arrival would be reason enough to clear the table. His cheeks hurt as he maintained a forced smile. How did beauty pageant contestants manage the constant simper?

Herman helped Lola to her chair and folded up the walker, placing it against the wall for the ease of the dietary staff before taking his own seat. "Well, now everybody's here!" Herman boomed in a jovial manner.

"Except Eunice," Gus lowered his article to correct the statement.

Without overthinking the situation, Jake plucked the article from his friend's fingers.

"Hey!" Jake's friend objected. "I wasn't done reading that!"

Right about now, Eunice's interference would be welcome. Maybe she would try to quiz the new arrival on her croquet skills. Jake folded the paper in half and shoved it into the envelope with the rest. Gus often didn't take no for an answer, which made him a good match for Eunice. He'd probably grab the envelope from him just because he could. The only thing for that was to slap the folder on his chair and sit on it, which he did. Acting as if this was something, he did all the time, he addressed Gus. "We needed to clear the table because dinner is on its way."

A large metallic clatter, along with a loud, "Oh dear!" came from the kitchen and captured the attention of the rubberneckers. Gus smirked and gave his head a slow shake. "There might be a slight delay."

That would be reason enough for Gus to demand the article back or rib Jake for a perceived insult. Time to turn on the charm. He made sure to allow his gaze to include both Lola and the new arrival. "I must say, I'm a lucky man to be surrounded by so much natural beauty."

Gus rubbed his hand over his bald pate and grinned. "I did try some wax on my head today. Nice of you to notice. Heard Yul Brynner used to wax his dome. I figured if it was good enough for Yul…"

Typical. It was as if they kept their roles from when they met over a half a century ago: Gus, the prankster; Herman, the solid nice guy; and Jake due to his non-talking became a female magnet. As a kid, he stuttered and dealt with it by practicing certain responses. Unfortunately, his practiced responses didn't always fit the occasion. Working with the senior sleuths taught him to improvise and oddly enough stuttering hadn't been an issue in a long time.

"No," Herman spoke, gesturing to himself. "He was talking about me and the new pomade I tried today. It's a glistening gel that picks up the light and makes your hair shine."

While it was unusual for Herman to tease, being married to Lola brought out the more playful side of his friend. It was all good since it smoothed over any strange behavior on his part. He decided to play along with their goofiness.

"Gus, your head is particularly fetching. The ladies at the next table can barely keep their eyes off you. Heads will roll when Eunice arrives."

The trio of women murmured something about being late, grabbed their purses and exited, all while trying not to look like they were rushing out of the room. That wasn't supposed to happen. Jake nodded at Herman. "Your pomade works. I was almost blinded when you sat down. Still, no one has introduced me to this lady of mystery."

"Hannah Conrad." She held out a long-fingered hand, which Jake shook with a light touch. Arthritis was no stranger to most of the residents, which often made firm handshakes a form of minor torture as opposed to a greeting.

"Pleased to meet you. Did you just move in today?" It would be the normal thing to say. By this time, Jake knew all the residents, even to the point of knowing which ones would trap him into listening to the same joke for about the thirtieth time. Others would pull out a wallet full of grandchildren snapshots as they extolled the talents of each child.

"Not yet," Hannah replied with a touch of humor in her tone. "I don't like to rush into things. I asked the administration if I could spend a day here to get a feel for it. Now, I realize nothing is ever as good as it's advertised to be. Found that out on plenty of vacations my husband and I took. We would think we were going to stay at some luxurious villa only to discover we had a hut with a leaky roof."

"Herman and I agreed to serve as her guides for the day," Lola announced in a tone that combined cheer and a touch of amusement. "We'll try not to get her into *too* much trouble."

They all chuckled at the possibility. It didn't go unnoticed that the administration hadn't asked Gus or Eunice to show the woman around. Eunice would say too much, and Gus might think a hand buzzer gag would be a great way to break the ice. Jake hadn't been asked, either. That stung a little, but the director may have assumed a woman would like another female's perspective. Never mind the absent husband who could veto the whole plan.

The mention of her husband might as well have been an oversized gong because the sound reverberated through Jake—not that he cared. It just made him wonder about the missing man. Was he sitting at home waiting to hear her report on the place? As an experienced sleuth, Jake should be able to extract the needed information. "Did your husband accompany you?"

His gaze went to the open door expecting a tall, distinguished man to step through and hail Hannah at any moment.

"Ah," she nodded in Jake's direction. "If you're looking for my husband, Houston, you must have amazing eyesight. We buried him at sea." Her nose crinkled, and she pursed her lips for the briefest of seconds. "That's not *totally* correct. Houston loved the sea. I always told him he was half merman. He joked I should return him to the water when he died. So, I did after he was cremated. We didn't tell anyone since you must get special permission to do so. Got one of those gallon size zipper bags and placed his ashes in it.

"Then I went on one of those dolphin cruises where the mammals never show. I spent most of my time hanging over the side of the boat releasing the ashes gently into the sea. The Captain must have thought I was seasick or desperate to see a fin. I like to think he got to swim with the dolphins, which was something Houston always wanted to do."

Lola pointed two fingers in Hannah's direction. "I like your style."

Truthfully, Jake did, too. Still, what good would it be if he used his best stuff on a woman he'd never see again? She'd find out the place wasn't as grand as the brochures made it out to be, although it was better than homes in the same price range. He knew because he investigated options when Gus first suggested about retiring to Greener Pastures. The best thing about Greener Pastures was if they thought you were sane and mobile, they left you alone do your own thing, which he could get behind. Even if she did stay, she was out of his league. For Pete's sake, her deceased husband's name was *Houston*.

"Me, too," Herman echoed his wife's sentiment about style. "Houston's an unusual name."

Hannah uttered a small chuckle. "I rarely used his actual name, Bertrand. Houston was a nickname he earned when he was working with…"

Before she could even finish, Jake mentally envisioned the words *space program*. Women judged each other on a variety of things, with half of them making no sense to him. The pecking order for men his age was a former job and money. A great job, such as being an astronaut, could skyrocket you to the top.

"NASA," Hannah concluded.

"You don't say." Lola put her hands on the table and leaned in Hannah's direction with an interested gleam. "Was he an astronaut?"

Why did he even bother to try? He didn't stand a chance with the women he liked. He should just accept that his fate was to be alone. Wasn't half the world single or something? He had read an article stating a similar sentiment. Either they were on purpose single, divorced, or widowed. It was something like forty-eight percent. His hands hovered near his ears, wanting to plug them up before she could mention her husband walked on the moon or something equally grand.

"He started the program." She gave a little sigh. "An injury to his eye kept him firmly planted on the ground. His degree in aeronautical engineering served him as one of those guys in Houston talking the astronauts through flight patterns and problems. Thus, the name, Houston. A *Bertrand* would never have been able to do that."

Who would? Jake shuddered. Most men would make sure they

had a nickname such as Bert or Bertie. Well, the man did have a cool nickname and a nice backstory to accompany it. No doubt the man had crafted toys for orphans and rescued wildlife from frigid waters, too.

The atmosphere changed suddenly. It wasn't much. Something someone might miss if they weren't alert to the little things. Conversation lowered a couple of notches and a few of the residents' frozen expressions reminded him of animals caught in the headlights. It made him wonder what would cause such a reaction. Oh yeah, he knew.

Eunice stood in the doorway with narrowed eyes, hands on the hips, staring at the diners. She marched over to the table, pulled out a chair, noticed Hannah, and put out her hand. "I'm Eunice."

"Hannah." They released hands and Hannah relaxed back into her chair, unaware Hurricane Eunice had just made landfall.

"You play croquet?" Eunice cocked her head rather like a bird listening for a worm. In her case, it was more likely juicy information. Gus had once mentioned one of her ears was better than the other.

"I used to." Hannah acknowledged with a wistful look. "As a girl, it was one of the few games my grandmother deemed acceptable for young girls."

"Yee haw!" Eunice clapped her hands together. "You're on my team. Sorry about the *yee haw*—it's a leftover from my square-dancing stint. Last quarter's activity," she announced with a shrug. "This time it is croquet. Seeing as you're an expert and all, maybe you can teach me the jargon."

"Wait!" Hannah held up a hand, possibly overwhelmed by

Eunice's steam roller attitude. "I'm just visiting to see if I *might* want to move here."

"Not live here?" Eunice repeated the words as if she didn't understand the language. Her shoulders slumped and she deflated the tiniest bit, surprising Jake. The woman he knew never got discouraged. Her eyes stared off into the distance and it was as if some tiny gears clicked into place, causing Eunice to straighten up and beam at Hannah. "You'll want to stay here. I'll guarantee it."

Then she took her petite size four foot and ground it into Jake's toes. Some messages didn't need to be spoken. If she expected him to squire Hannah around the center, her technique needed major work. Personally, he didn't feel as if he could sell Hannah on the idea of relocating.

Chapter Five

LUNCH ARRIVED IN plain white bowls brimming with fat dumplings, big chunks of chicken in a thick gravy, accompanied by a smaller bowl of coleslaw. Beside it on a small plate was a generous serving of Apple Betty. The dishes were a nice touch. In-room diners usually ate off a plastic tray with dividers reminiscent of school lunches. Jake knew Eunice expected him to sell the place for the sake of her croquet team. Sometimes, it was best to humor the woman because she did not give up—ever.

The dietary aides fluttered about the tables serving water, coffee, and iced tea. Since they knew who wanted what without asking, glasses were placed in front of the residents without any discussion except for an occasional *enjoy your meal* comment.

"Thank you." He acknowledged the aide who delivered his sweet tea.

"No problem," the middle-aged aide replied and nodded in Hannah's direction. "Can I get you iced tea, coffee, ice water, or lemonade?"

Lemonade? It had never been a choice before. Obviously, they were pulling out all the stops to impress the possible resident.

"Unsweetened iced tea, please. I'd love a diet lemonade, but most are made with sugar."

The aide hesitated before responding and shaking her head.

"Not sure what's in the lemonade. Tea might be your safer bet."

Jake took note of the surprise on the senior sleuths' faces. The addition of another beverage choice didn't go unnoticed. There were a few residents who had to have their daily soda, but either their relatives brought in a case or a delivery service handled it. Because it wasn't an option for everyone, they had to drink it in their rooms.

Jake lifted a spoonful of the fragrant entrée to his mouth and spoke before gobbling it. "The food is excellent. Thank goodness there's none of this diet food. A person should have a few pleasures in life. A man can grow up tired of hearing everything he *shouldn't* eat."

There were murmured agreements. Eunice's lips lifted the tiniest bit but didn't quite make a smile. Still, he knew it was a recognition of his effort. Major praise coming from Eunice.

Tea was handed off to Hannah, who thanked the aide. While the sleuths dug into their meal with gusto, Hannah used her phone to photograph her meal.

Jake's niece had commented on the trend of photographing your food, and then posting it on social media. If she wanted people to know, she could tell them. Not everyone had the same feelings, though.

"What's with the photos?" Eunice inquired, pointing to the phone.

"Nothing much," Hannah explained with a forced laugh. "It helps me keep track of what I eat. It's a lot easier when dinner comes out of a box, and I can snap the UPC code. Since I'm a diabetic, I use my phone app to keep track of my blood sugar. I input what I ate, and it tells me if I need to exercise or even take insulin. It's a little less intrusive than doing a finger prick at the table."

Jake slumped, replaying the remark about eating what he wanted with no diet food and other nonsense. What could have been worse to say to a diabetic? The best he could do was pretend he never said it. Most folks his age knew how to be courteous, which included not pointing out the dumb things someone said or inquiring about personal matters.

Eunice kept her attention on Hannah. "How long have you been a diabetic?" She made an expansive sweep of her arm, indicating most of the dining room. "A good bunch of these folks are type 2 diabetic. It's like it's something you get when you turn fifty, like a colonoscopy."

The possibility of dining in his own room on a plastic tray suddenly had appeal. Jake ladled another spoonful of dumplings into his mouth while trying to get Gus's attention since he was the one who exerted any influence over his sweetie. Gus had his head down and was busy making his food vanish. Could be he was avoiding eye contact with anyone. Then again, it was his usual mode of eating.

Hannah tittered. "I wish that's all it was. Unfortunately, I was diagnosed as a juvenile. My mother monitored everything that went into my mouth, which made eating a trial." She brandished her phone. "Using my app and monitoring my sugar, I can have a more realistic approach to food." She pointed to the dessert. "I might have a taste, but not all of it. To compensate, I'll walk more today and eat less tonight. It's something I've earned to live with." She pointed the phone in Eunice's direction. "I appreciate your direct approach."

Jake's spoon slipped from his fingers and clattered into his bowl. No one ever appreciated Eunice's direct approach. "You do?"

"Yes." Hannah arched her eyebrows. "Don't you?"

Nope. The newest addition to the group probably hadn't meant to set a trap, but it would snap closed on Jake all the same. Hannah would leave, and he'd have to deal with an irate Eunice. "Haven't given it much thought."

"Well, you should. I'm willing to bet Eunice gets answers because she doesn't pussyfoot around."

The woman in question slapped the table. "You're right. I do. I have the feeling we're going to be great friends."

Somehow the idea of Eunice buddying up with Hannah didn't ease Jake's mind one little iota, especially with Eunice's tendency to gossip. With *his* luck, he'd be her chief subject. This wasn't going well at all.

Talk swirled around him as he tried to think of a way to politely excuse himself. What he really should be doing is going over the articles and looking for a thread that connected them. It would help if he knew more about how Lyre worked. Who did she interact with daily? Maybe she said something to one of them before her disappearance. Anything out of the ordinary could still serve. Often, the mundane could be the smoking gun.

On a recent television show, they discovered a man was murdered because his staged suicide included whisky the man would never drink. It was enough to unravel the murder. What he needed was the one piece that didn't fit. The assumption was Lyre was killed because she was about to testify about the local mob. Could there have been a setup to fake her death for her own safety? What about DNA testing? Every way he turned birthed new questions.

"Earth to Jake," Gus hit a fork against his glass, which only made a dull thud against the plastic glass.

"What?" The word sounded more abrupt than he intended. Hannah raised curious eyes to his. Great! Now he sounded like a curmudgeon.

"Need an answer. Yes or no."

Because he hadn't been following the conversation, he didn't know the question. To ask would show his inattention. A *no* would confirm him as a grouch while a *yes* might rope him into agreeing to something he didn't like, which wasn't terrible. What if he agreed he preferred sherry or a chick flick? It wouldn't be the end of the world. "Yes?"

"Surprised," Gus remarked, while Eunice wrote on a preprinted form. She capped her pen and grinned.

"Got enough for a full team." She brandished the paper. "I need to get it to the activity director right away." She glanced at her food and back to Gus. "Don't let them take my food."

Jake watched as Eunice dashed off with more energy than a woman her age should have. He should ask what he just agreed to, but he had a sinking feeling he already knew.

"This sounds like this will be a fun place." Hannah grinned and speared a bit of Apple Betty. "Retirement has been rather dull for me. When Houston was alive, I used to attend the launches, but you know how the space program dropped out of the limelight. Even before my husband died, I thought I needed something to enliven my days. That's when I started working for a private investigator. The stories I could tell…"

Every one of the senior sleuths stopped eating and gazed at Hannah with various degrees of interest. Gus held up his hand and sighed. "I guarantee we'd love to hear your stories, but let's wait on

Eunice."

"A gentleman," Hannah mused. "Here I thought they had all disappeared."

Chapter Six

THE DIETARY AIDES bustled around the dining room removing empty dishes. In an actual restaurant, it would be the signal to leave. Jake had since learned the people who wanted to leave were the dietary aides themselves. They could after they did the lunch dishes.

Since most of the residents came to socialize, they often lingered over a cup of coffee or an iced tea. None of the sleuths were leaving if Hannah was holding court. The woman held up a finger and said, "Reminds me of a time my boss asked me to help out on a case. Something other than answering the phone and sending out invoices."

"Tell us more," Lola demanded in a husky whisper.

Hannah's shiny black hair held Jake's attention not in the way it normally would when a man spotted an attractive woman. Instead, he speculated if it was her real hair color or if she had a professional dye job, unlike his monthly do it yourself project with a box of drugstore color. Both Herman and Gus loved to rib him about misquoting beauty slogans such as *your hair's worth it* or *let your hair do the talking*. Sure, it was more than a broad hint there was nothing real about his hair. Still, Gus gained a sweetheart with no hair, while Herman had landed the pick of the center with his silver locks. Jake was still strolling the streets of Singlesville with his solid black style.

Although he hadn't made up his mind that he wanted to be part of a couple, he had accepted he didn't want to die alone, which loomed on the horizon as a real possibility. Laughter brought his attention back to the group.

Hannah held up her hands as she spoke. "I'll tell you about my adventures in investigating. Trust me. It's not much. Mike, my boss, needed someone in the bar to casually take photos while he contacted the target. He didn't come right out and say a senior citizen wouldn't attract too much attention, but I filled in what he didn't say. Possibly seniors were always taking random photos."

"Yeah, I know how it is," Herman said and acted as if he might say more. Jake faked a cough to catch his friend's eyes and shook his head. Sure, Hannah was easy to be around, which would lead to at least one sleuth wanting to compare adventures. A slip of the tongue would end their cold cases for good and might even cost Lance and Marcy their jobs.

Hannah missed the interaction between Herman and Jake or was polite enough not to mention it. Instead, she continued gesturing with her hands for emphasis. "It was back when we used cameras, not phones like people do today. I can see how a phone would have worked better. Mike strikes up a conversation with the guy who was collecting disability for being bed-bound and unable to work. The rumor was he had a regular stool at this dive bar. When he got liquored up enough, he usually started dancing, gyrating his way through the crowds and occasionally making it up to the postage stamp stage."

Gus hooted. "I can't do that, and I'm not on bed rest!"

"Exactly." Hannah agreed and pantomimed searching through

her purse and holding her fingers together in a loose rectangle. "Anyhow, I'd just pulled my camera out of my bag when a couple spots me. They thought I was one of those roving photographers who takes your snapshot, then sells it to you at the end of the night. They were very vocal about me taking a snapshot of them."

"What did you do?" Jake asked, finding himself caught up in the story even though he should be in his room going over the articles. He shouldn't be checking out Hannah, if that was her real name. He narrowed his eyes in her direction, considering the possibility the woman might be a plant—someone sent in to uncover the senior sleuths. The only issue with the scenario is who would do such a thing? Finding the origin of conspiracies was always an issue. Maybe he should just listen. Television sleuths unraveled cases simply by listening, along with obvious clues.

Perhaps noting Jake's strange expression, inattention, or both, Hannah paused and waited until she had his focus. "Well, I noticed they were fairly young, so I asked for their IDs. Suddenly, they slipped out of the bar before I could say another word. I did get photos of the dancing man. I could have told my too-young-to-be-in-the-bar lovebirds that no photographers roamed dive bars, but it might have taken too long to do so."

"Smart," Eunice quipped, with an approving expression.

High praise from the stubborn woman, which made Jake do a double-take. Compliments were not something Eunice handed out freely. His lips pulled down a touch as he contemplated her motivations. She was still planning on Hannah being a part of the croquet team. With any luck, she could be a decent player, which would help because none of the rest of them were.

"I thought so," Hannah added with a chuckle. "It wasn't too bad for something I made up on the spot. Most of the time, I just answered phones and occasionally typed up notes, which made me feel a bit like I was on a case. Most of the jobs he went out on were pretty run-of-the-mill, including disability fraud, cheating spouses, and he also ran down high-ticket stolen items, usually taken from museums."

"Ooh," Herman interjected. "It sounds like the movie about stolen art work. Was it like that?"

"Not exactly." Hannah's hands folded as her eyes rolled upward. "The police didn't necessarily go chasing down folks on the museum's say-so. They wanted proof. Mike got the police the information they needed."

This was more down Jake's alley or should he say, the Senior Sleuths' alley. The police gave up on Lyre because they didn't have any evidence. "How did he find out who stole what?"

Residents had been leaving while Hannah talked. Most stole a curious peek as they exited. One resident remained, but his heavy snoring announced he'd already merged into his afternoon nap. Still, their newest guest twisted in her seat to see if anyone was behind her. There wasn't. Only the sounds of the industrial dishwasher and snoring filled the dining room. One hand went up to her mouth, shielding her from a possible lip-reader hidden in the wood paneling.

"I don't know everything Mike did. He didn't tell me much. He'd call people and pretend to be someone else, as if he were calling for a job reference, or from a utility company—whatever place might need personal data. He did the social media thing, reverse lookups, searched arrest reports, and sometimes even used those public record searches in a pinch. What worked best for him were informants. Mike did seedy, down on his luck really well. He'd find out the favorite bar of art thieves and hang out there for a while. He always warned me it didn't work to make your move too soon. It would be suspicious to show up in a bar and start asking about stolen paintings. The man was brilliant. He always had a backstory."

An uneasy sensation regarding all wouldn't end well for Mike crept up Jake's spine. He remembered Hannah enjoyed working for Mike, but didn't anymore. It was obvious she could still work, which meant the problem had to be with Mike.

Before he could ask, Eunice cleared her throat. "Mike sounds sharp, but I got the feeling you're going to tell us about when he wasn't."

A heavy sigh escaped Hannah. "You're so right. It was the last case. Museum theft. The museum was convinced it was an inside job, but there was nothing to implicate any of the staff. Police did investigate. Mike uncovered some information that one of the guards had been a decent art student, which set off his radar. Told me he was going to meet a guy at this hellhole that served beer in cans, which probably prevented listeria or salmonella."

A former art student would probably love working in a museum. "Why would an art student set off a radar?"

Hannah stared at him uncomprehendingly, blinked a couple of times, and forced a laugh. "As the kids would say, my bad. I forgot to mention the stolen pictures were being replaced by forgeries. It's hard to say how long this went on. They brought in an appraiser for insurance purposes for a traveling show, which was when they discovered several of their precious masterpieces were forgeries. It's rather like finding the horse you've had in the barn for months wasn't the one you bought."

Normally Jake liked to pride himself on how he could follow clues, but he was missing this one. "Good chance most people who work at the museum have some history in art. Why would this make a big difference?"

Instead of replying, Hannah rummaged through her purse and pulled out a handkerchief and shook it out. She gave a little sniff and dabbed at the edges of her eyes. "All I know is Theo, the guy Mike suspected, tried to hide his art background while others would extol it as a reason to work there. He also changed his name. In the end, I have no clue what happened since Mike ended up shot in the back and no one's talking."

The Senior Sleuths exchanged glances with each other, trying to convey their reactions to the latest reveal. Spectacular and surprising as it sounded, Jake had his doubts if any of it had happened. He needed to get back to his room and attempt to verify if any of it was true. One thing his decades on this side of the grass taught him was people lie for multiple reasons, including creating a more interesting tale.

His gaze traveled over his friends, who appeared intent on the story. His departure might cause verbal speculation, even some ribbing by Gus. What he needed was a decent excuse. Most would fake illness, saying they had a headache or a stomach ache. Jake shifted in his chair, anxious to depart but discarding the sickness plan. Even though Hannah might not be the person she pretended to be, she was still the most interesting female he'd encountered in years. No reason to sour any romantic chances he might have by getting labeled incorrectly as a sickly person. Women preferred healthy men unless they had some desire to hover and mother. From what he'd heard so far, no one would refer to Hannah as a hoverer.

It left him with nothing as an exit route. An odd *burbling* sounded, causing Jake to pivot his head in search of the source. Most of the senior sleuths started patting pockets to discover if their phone could be the culprit. Jake did likewise and discovered it was *his* phone. An image of his nephew making a face identified the caller.

"Oh, it's my great-nephew. I need to take this." He pushed away from the table while answering the phone. "Hello?"

He listened as his great-nephew regaled him with a tale about his history teacher being the target of a practical joke, which involved switching names on student papers to show he never actually read the work. Normally, he'd have discouraged the antics, but it sounded like the man had it coming. Before he knew it, he was back in his room. Better yet, his exit from the group would provoke no comments.

Chapter Seven

Voices of passing people and the squeaking of a medicine cart slipped through Jake's slightly ajar door. Most residents kept their doors open or slightly cracked to signal they were open to company. A closed door meant the resident was asleep, possibly dressing, or up to something interesting such as a meeting of the Senior Sleuths. So far, the closed door wasn't as discouraging as one might think since the activity director hunted them down wherever they might be. To her credit, she knew who was alert, mobile, and could be coerced into lending a hand with her latest project.

It could be worse, he reminded himself as he spread out the copies of the articles by Lyre. At least he had something to occupy his time as opposed to watching endless reruns of shows that were no longer made. The paper rasped as he sorted the articles by date. Since they were only copies, it should be okay to write on them. He picked up the highlighter on his table that he sometimes used for bingo. What he needed to find were the names of folks who might have a reason to get rid of her. Of course, people were always quick to finger the mob for a crime, then pretty much forget about it. Not sure if they felt the mob was untouchable or maybe just an easy answer for any unsolved crime.

He uncapped his yellow marker and started highlighting names. Those she exposed probably suffered severe consequences along with public humiliation. If various forensic shows had taught him anything, it was those put behind bars could hold a grudge for a long time. Even though it would be natural to assume the case where she was about to testify was the best reason for her disappearance, what if it wasn't?

A spiral wire notebook rested on his table. Since it was just him and he mostly ate in the dining room, he never cleared his table, which also served as his desk. It wasn't like he'd whip up a meal for a friend. With both Herman and Gus paired off, he felt lonelier than ever in a building full of people of similar age. Gus had encouraged him to relocate with the promise of getting all the war buddies together. The same line brought Herman in, which was quite a feat since he was more than two states away. What he thought they'd do besides hang out and reminisce wasn't clear at the time. In the back of his mind, maybe he supposed it would be a chance to start again—be himself, which would be hard to explain to most because he felt like he'd fallen into a role created for him when he first joined the service.

His taciturn manner was taken for worldly wisdom when he was only an Indiana farm boy with no clue what to say. His height, trim physique, and dark hair caused some women to remark on his resemblance to a certain popular movie star. He didn't see it. That guy was smooth, while he was awkward like a day-old colt with too-long legs.

Still, it gave him a little guidance on how to be and he tried to model his behavior on the movie star or at least the dashing characters he portrayed, but that only worked for a little while. Once he dropped the mask, women were disappointed that he was an ordinary guy without the trappings of a movie star, such as a private jet or an expensive Italian sports car. It was a bit of a bait and switch. His ex-wife married him on a whim, not really knowing the man behind the façade and was disappointed once she met the real Jake.

A heavy sigh escaped. His goal with the move to Greener Pastures was to become more authentic, as the kids might say. The only problem was Herman and Gus expected him to be the old Jake, who kept silent except to dole out heavy-handed compliments to the women. He didn't want to be that guy. Senior Sleuths helped some, allowing his friends to discover he was more than an aging Lothario.

Switching from highlighter to pen, he flipped open the spiral notebook. Once he found a clean page, he wrote POSSIBLE SUSPECTS BEHIND LYRE'S DISAPPEARANCE. Jake wrinkled his nose at the words, remembering his great-nephew told him all caps was considered yelling. Maybe there should be some shouting involved with an investigative reporter vanishing right when she was going to drop the hammer on some dirty doings. He drew a bold line down the center of the paper. On one side he wrote the names of people she'd fingered. He'd have to follow up to see if they had done time or were in prison when she went missing. Even though most assumed she was dead, he refused to do so until it could be proven. Maybe Lyre was tucked away someplace with a bad case of amnesia. A bit farfetched, he knew, but what was wrong with hoping for the best?

On the other side of the line, he wrote those of interest. First on the list was the sister Lorelei. From what little Lance told them, the sister's interest was on the parrot Lyre kept. He'd heard those birds could cost a pretty penny. There may have been something about the bird trade out of South America being closed due to the possibility of disease. It would make the parrot even more valuable. He pursed his lips as he considered the possibility of a sibling knocking off another for a pricey pet. Family members had killed for less. After giving the matter some reflection, he shook his head. If Lorelei had wanted the bird, she could have taken it as opposed to waiting for the police to show up at her door. Still, it might be worth visiting the sister, which would require an excuse to get inside the front door. With people being a tad more paranoid than years ago, he needed something believable.

Various ideas came and went as he discarded them as being unworkable. No one took the paper anymore. Any type of sales or evangelizing would keep the door closed to him. What he needed was a sure-fire way to get inside. Most salespeople offered gifts—but nothing big that would outweigh the value of the product being offered. What would interest the woman?

Dealing with the unknown woman reminded him of the mysterious Hannah, who he'd vowed to check out. It would only take a few seconds to see if his hunch that the woman was lying through her teeth rang true. All the other sleuths were lapping up what she had to say. His lips pulled down into a frown when he realized the response he'd get if he mentioned things just didn't feel right. What he needed was proof.

His first place to look was social media. There were plenty of Hannah Conrads, but none that bore any resemblance to the one Herman and Lola were currently escorting. Dozens of articles about an attractive couple named Hannah *and* Conrad. No help there. An iconic lightbulb practically glowed over his head as he considered a different approach. If she had been married to someone in the space program, it would be easy enough to uncover the info. After all, there were a limited number of such individuals.

Astronaut names came up on his search, including a few cosmonaut names which he immediately rejected as he scoured the list for Conrad. There *was* one! His upper teeth bit down on his bottom lip as he considered he may have misjudged the woman. Doubt came from her behavior of being so lively and forthcoming. He'd almost call it acting. A good sleuth digs a little deeper. The information identified the Astronaut as Pete Conrad, with the first name being in quotations. Maybe the man had several nicknames. He clicked on the link, which took him to an encyclopedia article on the man.

Using his mouse, he enlarged the words for easy reading. No mention of the man's name being Bertrand. Surely a wife would know her husband's name. He had been very active in NASA but died, which would make Hannah a widow. So far, fifty percent of her story was correct. He kept reading until he got to the family section where he read his wife's name was Jane—didn't even sound the least like Hannah. Part of him secretly rejoiced she hadn't been married to an astronaut. Another part reminded him that she was a liar.

A single knock sounded before the door opened under Gus's open palm. "Whatcha doing?"

Rather than admit he been checking out Hannah, he turned to face Gus. "Trying to figure out a way to see Lorelei, Lyre's sister."

Instead of responding, Gus stroked his chin thoughtfully and moved closer. He peeked over Jake's shoulder to peer at the computer.

"Checking out the NASA connection, I see."

"Wouldn't you?" He schooled his face to be non-expressive, which would be the cool, collected response of the Jake most knew.

Gus lifted his bushy eyebrows in acknowledgment, "Maybe...if I had a romantic interest in the woman, I'd do the same. Space Program guy trumps fighter pilot every time. Still, there're no aeronautic engineers at Greener Pastures. You *should* stand a chance." He chortled as if he had made a huge joke.

Not funny but correct in more ways than Jake liked to admit. He inhaled audibly and pondered if he should mention what he found. Gus, despite his love of practical jokes, was a good sounding board. "There's no mention of a Hannah Conrad being married to an astronaut. There is no Bertrand or Houston Conrad."

"So?" Gus picked up the notebook and held it at arm's length trying to read it.

"It means she's lying."

Gus lowered the notebook to look at Jake and smirked. "Lying is such a harsh word. Women take back their maiden names all the time. It's something to do with getting in touch with their roots or who they are as opposed to who they married. Not totally sure about all that. You'll have to ask Eunice for the exact reasons."

Asking Eunice anything wasn't something he'd choose to do. A maiden name would make it much harder to research her astronaut spouse. There couldn't be that many men named Bertrand in the space program. "I'll need to do a little more research."

"Bird inspector!" Gus blurted the words.

"What?" Half the time, Jake felt like he came in in the middle of a movie when talking to Gus.

"You know." Gus bobbed his head. "You wanted to know how we could get into Lyre's sister's house. She has the parrot. We could pose as inspectors."

"That's…" The word *ridiculous* stuck in his mouth as he considered his current sum of possibilities. He had zero ways of getting his foot in the door. "Doable. Maybe they register parrots? We need a type of organization. Perhaps we can drop off some expensive parrot seed or something."

Gus snorted. "Why does every idea involve spending money?"

He had a point. Every cold case they had solved did involve some money even if was just for gas. "It is what it is. Remember that Jim Rockford, television private eye, had a daily rate plus expenses."

"Yeah," Gus agreed. "All we have are expenses and no one footing our bill."

Chapter Eight

THE AFTERNOON SUN beamed through the open blinds, spotlighting Gus's bald pate. Jake chose not to mention it. One thing he had learned from his decades of being on earth was everything didn't need to be verbalized. There were even times his taciturn nature served him well or at least kept him out of trouble. When he did talk, he sometimes ended up saying the wrong thing. That's why he settled on lame and hackneyed lines. They seem to be what most females like to hear. A compliment on appearance had most of the women grinning like Gus. Praise on his friend's outfit would fall flat, especially since he wanted recognition for his plan.

"I don't know, Gus. Is there such a thing as a parrot inspector?" Jake pinched the bridge of his nose. His friend was often like a preschooler showing boundless energy when he concocted a plan. Always ready to charge full speed ahead, never hesitating, which, on a couple of occasions, had ended up with requiring police assistance.

"Don't know." His bushy brows lowered as he contemplated the matter. "Maybe there should be. Birds carry diseases, you know. Heard about it on the news. Maybe a health inspector or something."

A flash of reflected light drew Jake to the window in time to see a familiar car drive by. It reminded him of Lance's sedan. Maybe he'd get a reprieve from having to explain why pretending to be a health inspector wasn't the best plan. "Remember, people aren't going to open a door to someone who is going to cause problems. Just the name *health inspector* implies you might hit them with a fine or even take their bird away. Can't see it working. Besides, we don't even have Lorelei's address. We don't even know if the bird is still alive. I've heard tropical birds can live a long time, but how old was it when Lyre first got it? How could we explain how we tracked it down to Lorelei without seeming all creepy?"

"That's a problem," Gus agreed and crossed his arms. His lips twisted to one side, then his nose wrinkled, signifying he was giving the matter some thought. Finally, he held up one finger and his eyes lit up. "I got it!"

Jake knew he'd probably regret asking, but he wanted to know. "Okay, what is it?"

"We don't know we're at Lorelei's house."

This was starting to sound like the old Abbott and Costello comedy sketch about who's on first. Jake cleared his throat. "We'd be *at* Lorelei's home, knocking on her door. How would we not know we were there? What reason could we give for our arrival?"

"We were looking for Lyre's house and since the sisters have the same last name, we decided to check." He waved his lightly fisted hands in the air in triumph. "We tell her we're part of the parrot party club, and it's the parrot's birthday. We brought presents, too." Aware that Jake might say something, Gus hurried to finish. "Lyre signed up for the parrot club a couple of years ago."

Parrot club was a little far-fetched, but plenty of people signed up for birthday clubs at fast-food restaurants. They usually received a card in the mail for a free meal or dessert. No one received a home visit though. "I'm not sure if they have the same last name. Besides, you don't think the parrot club would have heard about Lyre's disappearance?"

"Please." Gus dropped his hands and inserted them into his pockets. "It's a small business. We don't have time to check the news to see if any of our members are mentioned in it. We're fortunate that Lyre listed her sister as a second contact."

Surprisingly, Jake found himself nodding at the explanation. Most applications for free stuff didn't ask for a second person. The entire idea behind free stuff was getting people to buy more stuff, which meant they might offer another perk to get a second contact name. If Lyre and Lorelei weren't on the best terms—as implied by the case notes—she might have used Lorelei's name to get free stuff and irritate her sister while she was at it. Of course, it was all hypothetical but felt possible.

"What about last year? We didn't come by last year?"

"Ah, that was a bad year, I'm sorry to say. I hired my grandson, and he just wasn't dependable. That's why I decided on making the visits myself this year. Seemed like the only decent thing to do."

Gus's downturned mouth and heavy sigh carried just the right amount of regret. Hollywood missed out on a possible star. Jake shook his head, reminding himself how past plans had panned out. The fact he was still standing meant he survived them, but he'd had his doubts during them. His best response would be to stall. "Throw your grandson under the bus."

"No need to mention I can almost see it working out, especially if we're carrying a basket of bird goodies. We don't even have the sister's address, though. She might not even live nearby."

Before he could say anymore, he heard Lance addressing a staff member by name outside the room door. The fact he knew people by name meant the man was either a genius at remembering names or was here way too much. It surprised Jake that people didn't wonder about the detective's frequent visits. The staff probably assumed he was a nice guy, which was true.

A lively knock sounded followed by Lance calling out, "Anyone home?"

"Come on in!" Gus responded, never mind it not being his room. The door opened a little wider as Lance inserted himself, then he quietly closed it.

"Here I am, back as promised with copies of the file for every-one." He brandished an oversized envelope in his right hand. "Nevertheless," he arched his eyebrows, "I feel obliged to say you should pick another file. There is very little to go on, and I worry about the mob connection."

Gus made a grab for the envelope and pulled it out of Lance's hand, carrying it to the table and spilling it open on top of the highlighted articles. It was hard to know what the man was looking for as he held up each paper and peered at it from arm's length. Despite Gus's claim that he didn't need glasses, he could have benefitted from some readers. "Aha! Found it."

Lance and Jake asked in unison, "What?"

"The sister's address," Gus announced with his chin up and his shoulders pushed back. He acted as if he had found a treasure map or the cure for cancer.

"Ah," Lance drew out the word. "How would you approach the sister without raising suspicions?"

Gus put one hand on his hip reminiscent of Eunice when she was ready to dress someone down. "I don't tell you how to do your job. You don't tell me how to do mine."

Just when Jake was certain the detective's raised eyebrows couldn't go any higher, they did. "Excuse me?" Lance said with an unaccustomed edge.

It sounded like it would be up to Jake to explain and defuse any misunderstanding. He held up his hand as if it were a white flag. "Hey, no issues here." His forced chuckle sounded as fake as it was. "Gus, here, had an idea we could show up with a basket of bird goodies as part of the bird birthday club that Lyre had signed up for before her disappearance."

It might have been unfair to place the whole idea on his friend, but technically it was Gus who thought they could be parrot inspectors. Jake's contribution was they had to have a gift since people always wanted free stuff. Many a vacuum salesperson got in the front door by offering a six-pack of soda for a free demo. Surely Lance would laugh it off and that would be the end of it. They would have to go back to highlighting articles and web searches.

Lance held his index finger to his mouth for a few seconds. "You know, that *could* work. Especially with you two. Younger people would never pull it off, but a couple of seniors like yourself would still believe in personal service."

"Woo hoo!" Gus exclaimed and thumped his chest. "Remember, it's all my idea!"

"I came up with the gift angle," Jake pointed out. "Now all we have to do is get the bird stuff for the basket, assemble it, find out when Lorelei is home, and convince Herman to drive us."

"Ahem," Lance cleared his throat. "I think I should drive you guys. Maybe I could review appropriate behavior as we go. If you get in trouble, I'll be there, too." He checked his watch. "I'll be back by six-thirty with the basket."

Both Gus and Jake promised to be ready and bid Lance goodbye. After he left, Gus turned to Jake and shook his head. "Did you hear him? He's going to prep us as if we might do something wrong."

Chapter Nine

AFTER LANCE LEFT, Jake moved to reorder the case file papers dumped on his table. As usual, Lance had made copies for each member of the sleuthing team as opposed to making them share. The man knew them so well. Even though he could hear Gus's grumbling, Jake tuned out the specifics. So far, they didn't have much on Lyre, and he needed to start somewhere, especially if he planned on interviewing the sister. Sure, he'd refer to it as just a visit from the parrot club, which happened to be owned by two chatty octogenarians. It should work. Younger folks tended to think of their elders as grumpy or overly gregarious, rambling on about everything from the weather to current events. While conversation wasn't his strong point, he could fake it.

"Hey!" Gus raised his voice, possibly aware he was being ignored. "Did you hear what I said?"

"Of course, I did. How could I not when you're loud enough?" Jake answered as he compiled the stapled copies into one pile while clearing a space for his notebook and highlighted articles. Picking up a pen, he hooked a foot around a chair leg and pulled it out with a slight smile. It was a small thing, but it made him happy to still be agile enough to pull out a chair with his foot without falling on his face.

Apparently, those Tai Chi classes he was taking in the morning were paying off. Even though the instructor never came right out and said it, most had figured out the classes were offered free of charge to improve residents' balance and prevent frivolous lawsuits when grandma or grandpa took a tumble. Less tumbles equaled fewer lawsuits.

"What did I say, then?" Gus leaned over the table, dropping close enough to breathe his eucalyptus-tinged breath into Jake's face.

Great. He was caught in a lie and he needed to wiggle his way out without hurting his friend's feeling. Technically, he *was* listening because he was aware that Gus's lips were flapping. The fact he was focused on the file contents as opposed to the actual conversation was another matter. Knowing Gus, there were about three main topics he defaulted to, which included Eunice, food, and being treated like a child. Eunice wasn't here and lunch was good which meant it had to be the third one. Since Lance just left, it could also be related to the detective.

"Lance is just doing his job. He's protecting all of us." Jake offered up the vague statement like a blindfolded dart player aiming for a board's last known general location.

"Yeah…" Gus agreed with a sigh and dropped into a chair. He rested his head in his hands. "It just makes me feel old."

"You *are* old," Jake couldn't help pointing out and got a cold stare for it. "I'm old, too. Besides, if we weren't capable, we wouldn't be able to help on these cold cases. In a city of thirty thousand plus people of various ages, how many civilians do you think are helping with cold cases?"

His friend settled for a shrug.

"I'll tell you." He held up one hand with fingers spread wide.

"Five. That's it. If it were a thing, we wouldn't have to be so secretive about it." The possibility of Eunice blabbing the Sleuth activities to Hannah to appear important poked at him. "Um, your sweetheart…" he started awkwardly, not knowing how to frame the question without being insulting.

"Forget about it," Gus mumbled. "I know Eunice loves a good gossip, but she also knows what not to talk about. She holds it close like a special treasure that she has and others don't. You can count on her to keep her lips zipped about the sleuth activities."

Jake only wished he could feel as confident. He pulled his notebook closer, flipped to a new page, and labeled every other line with numbers.

"What are you doing?" his friend prompted.

"Trying to think of questions we can ask Lorelei without appearing too odd." He puzzled on what would reveal information while appearing ordinary. Next to number one he wrote, *What was the parrot's name?* It should be on the parrot's birthday card, but the sister might accept they forgot the name because they were old or simply didn't put the name on the envelope. It might help if they found out the parrot's name, then found references to it, especially if she'd named it after someone important in her life.

Gus placed his hand on the page. "I got it. We could ask her if there was anyone who wanted to kill her sister."

The wide grin announced his friend thought this was an obvious question. To some it might be, but not to the parrot party club owners who knew nothing about Lyre's disappearance. Jake shook his head before replying. "We don't want direct questions that might make her suspicious. We might try some parrot talk and allow

Lorelei to tell us stuff without realizing it."

"Parrot talk? Are you the bird whisperer now?" Gus inquired with a dismissive sniff.

"No. I *do* watch television, especially on Saturday mornings when that vet show is on. Parrots tend to pick out their feathers when they are distressed. Sometimes, they're aggressive. Other times, they won't eat or talk as much and perform repetitive behavior. Lorelei will immediately tell us she's not Lyre and her sister isn't there, possibly hoping that'll get rid of us. It's important to listen to how she says it."

"Got it." Gus held up a thumb to indicate comprehension. "If she breaks into tears, then maybe she actually cared for her sis."

"Possibly." Jake tapped his pen on his friend's hand to get him to move it, which he did. "I'm more interested in her explanation about her sister. Will she say her sister is dead? She might say her sister is missing. Could be she might say her sister isn't there, indicating nothing."

"Don't forget she could just slam the door in our faces or possibly not open it at all."

"There is that. I can only work with what I know currently. If we're able to see the bird, I can make a visual inspection asking if the bird was pulling out its feathers when she got it. I'm not sure how long the bird was alone, but I'm sure it was distressed being locked up without food or water. Then I could mention that sometimes birds are impacted by the owner's emotions. I might ask if Lyre was afraid of something."

"I thought the sisters weren't close," Gus pointed out.

"Could be," Jake conceded even though it galled him to do so. It sort of ruined his plan about questioning the sister. "People say stuff like that all the time, especially when they don't want to talk to the police. Not being close could mean a lot of stuff, too. Maybe they didn't do lunch or share clothes, but they did have a general idea of what was happening in each other's lives. Lorelei could be good for supplying a friend's name or a boyfriend. They might know more."

Gus coughed, then fished a cough drop out of his pocket. As he unwrapped it, he nodded in Jake's direction. "Good plan, I'll give you that. What if there isn't a parrot?"

Even though the possibility killed his plan, the thought *had* lingered in the back of his mind. Jake blew out an audible breath. "We'd be pretty much where we are right now."

"At a dead end," Gus concluded glumly and held up his index finger. "We know her laptop was missing. Along with any thumb drives, desktop computers, printers, and any pertinent information into her investigations. The assumption is someone took it. Obviously, someone or someones who didn't want the information to get out."

Paper rasped as Gus flipped through the case file copy. He bent the pages to display photos of the apartment. The place was a little sloppy, but not trashed as if someone had ransacked it. There was a close-up on the doorknob and lock. "No obvious signs of a break-in. If there *was* a break-in, you'd think the landlord or neighbors would have noticed."

Jake leaned forward to stare at the photo and finally picked up another sheaf of notes, turned to the same page, and carried it to the window where the light was better. "I wish we had the original file since the photos would have been better than these copies, but with

Marcy being back at work, there's no way to justify missing case files." He turned the paper until he got the best light on it. "No signs of any lock picking or forced entry. That means she could have known him or her and let the person in."

He flipped through the rest of the photos, which showed no signs of a fight or any blood splatter. "If she was killed, it had to be elsewhere."

"I think she was leaving," Gus interjected with a sage nod. "There's mention of the house being practically empty with half a soda and part of a takeout pizza in the fridge."

"Could have been not much of a cook."

Gus stood and walked into the kitchenette area and opened the full-sized fridge, displaying the contents which included a loaf of bread, various condiments, water bottles, a couple of beers, and an opened roll of summer sausage along with two withered apples. "You're not much of a cook and you got more in your fridge than she did."

"True enough. It's looking like Lyre was preparing to run. The question is if she ever got to or not. You'd think if she started packing up stuff to move, someone might notice, like her landlord, who might wonder if she was skipping out on her rent."

Gus added, "Good point. He might be worth talking to, but I doubt we can use the birthday parrot club."

"You're right. This case has more questions than answers. No wonder it was shelved." Every step forward resulted in two steps backward. What he needed was to take a walk and clear his head. "Gus, I'm going for a stroll. You can meet me back here at around six. It's imperative that Eunice does not tag along."

"No worries," Gus patted his chest. "I know how to handle her.

Handling explosive ordinances wasn't the only thing I learned in the army."

Hand to hand combat wouldn't work with Eunice since he knew the woman would not hesitate to fight dirty. Gus had to be referring to something else. He picked up the case file copies and his note-book to secure in the lockbox under his bed. Anyone with a lick of sense would take precautions. That meant he had to be super cautious. Would Lyre have used cloud storage, or would that have been hackable, too?

He turned the key in the lock and pushed the box under the bed. Normally, when he left his room, he locked it up behind him. Still, the staff had a key if they needed to get into his room. It made him wonder if maybe they should memorize the case details and burn the files, rather like the old television show where the mission tape disintegrated after being heard.

Another mystery awaited him. Jake checked his cell phone to make sure he had enough power. Observing his actions, Gus nudged him. "Going to bump into the lovely Hannah?"

"It *could* happen," he offered without giving out any details. More likely he was going to figure out who the woman was before she hoodwinked any of his friends.

Chapter Ten

POLKA MUSIC FLOWED underneath the doors of the activity center. Jake's feet carried him as far from the doors as possible without running into the wall. Caution served since he'd experienced more than once getting pulled into an activity he'd eschewed by choice. The ratio of men to women at Greener Pastures was 1 to 4, which sounded good. The downside of being coherent, mobile, and a reasonably good dancer was that he had a plethora of female dancing partners.

Courtesy demanded he dance with any woman who wanted to dance. If that wasn't enough, age had made some of the ladies a bit more assertive and would ask him to dance, not waiting around to *be* asked. Add in his friends, who would urge him to ask the ladies tapping their toes and gazing forlornly at couples twirling around the floor. Even when residents were just practice dancing, Jake was pulled in to participate.

The offer to dance sometimes caused his partner to mistake his intentions. Sometimes, he had women yelling at each other, declaring he was their partner. Herman loved to joke about this, but as a married man, he didn't have to dance with anyone other than his wife, Lola. While his friends teased Jake about being sought after, he knew better. Most of the residents didn't really have the opportunity to meet anyone besides those who lived at the center. While the women outnumbered the men, the males who would dance were even fewer.

Gus joked if Jake couldn't find a sweetie here, he wouldn't find one anywhere. The possibility made him sigh as the music picked up. No way was he going to get pulled into a class. It could be the local clogger club showing off their moves or even elementary students acting out a school play. Either way, he didn't want any part of whatever it was. Getting a snapshot of the mysterious Hannah topped his to-do list. He'd upload it to his computer and do a reverse image search.

He stumbled across the option when looking for ways to identify a photo. Tons of identification apps, including ones where you could take a single snap of a plant and find out what it was, were available. Another app allowed you to snap a picture of merchandise and would provide information on how to buy it.

Already, he knew there was no Hannah Conrad married to an Astronaut Pete Conrad. Maybe she should give Gus's theory about Hannah using her maiden name the benefit of the doubt. He twisted his lips to one side and considered it for a brief second. "Nope."

His gut told him something was off about the visitor. Women were always credited with an intuition that helped them avoid tricky, often dangerous situations, while men relied on something a little less ethereal. An uneasy digestive system had saved him a multitude of grief, sometimes involving money, and on a few occasions, it may have saved his life.

Instead of a huge knot in his stomach, he had a mild niggling tickle at the back of his neck. It might be good to find out who Hannah really was. If she was a small-time hustler, what did the woman expect to get here? Greener Pastures was far from the mansions of the rich and famous.

While some residents entered the center at the suggestion of their families or physicians, many like himself made the choice to live in a community as opposed to living alone. As an independent individual, he controlled his movements and his life. If he chose, he could leave tomorrow. The thought didn't cheer him as much as he thought it should. Sure, it would demonstrate his independence, but at what cost?

His long legs carried him to a series of windows that looked out on the courtyard area. Red and blue benches squatted on the patchy lawn about every ten feet or so. Large potted palms and a few shorter pots of mums enlivened the area. One overgrown dogwood contributed meager shade when the sun hit just right. Jake could attest to that personally after trying to make use of its limited coverage while watching a prior shuffleboard tournament.

A few lengths of cement bore shuffleboard triangles with painted numbers inside. Not too far from the cement stood Herman, Lola, Hannah, and Eunice with a mallet in her hand, possibly testing the visitor's actual croquet skills.

Perfect. Jake pulled out his phone and chose the camera option. The screen revealed a group of people with very little of Hannah showing. Herman hogged most of the screen with his height and heft.

Jake's great-nephew always tried to keep Jake up to date on his electronics. He'd even shown Jake how to use the camera and make small objects bigger with the telephoto lens. Something about using his fingers. He rubbed his fingers across the screen with a sweeping motion with no result. His lips pulled down as he stared at his phone.

"Cheez and crackers." He growled the words, knowing good and well this phone could do close-up shots. He had done it before.

"What's wrong?" a feminine voice asked.

Jake turned slightly and met the inquisitive stare of a twenty-something nursing aide. It would be embarrassing to admit he was trying to take a photo of the group in the courtyard. None of the sleuths would know how to do it either.

Choices. He swallowed hard and held up his phone. "I forgot how to make the phone take a close-up shot. My great-nephew showed me at one time…" He shrugged his shoulders, leaving the obvious unsaid.

"Okay." The aide glanced past the phone into the courtyard. "Ah, I see." She giggled before holding out her hand for the phone.

Once situated in her left hand, she put her thumb and forefinger of her right hand together against the screen, then slowly separated them, making the image larger. "You can do this as many times as you need, making the people larger. I'll warn you the bigger it is the blurrier it gets. I think it's sweet you're trying to get a photo of your crush. Which one is she?"

"There's no crush," Jake informed her brusquely. Even though he wasn't familiar with the helpful aide, it didn't stop her from talking. The last thing he needed was the staff gossiping about him.

"Uh-huh," The woman grinned at him. "That's how my grandpa and grandma met."

"What?" Jake was certain he'd missed part of the conversation.

"Grandma was coming out of the church…" she started conversationally.

Jake cut his eyes to the courtyard window, worried he might lose his chance for a photo, but he couldn't duck out of a story that was being related for his benefit. His lips turned up slightly in a forced smile, and he nodded for her to continue. "Church, huh?"

"Yes…" The aide nodded, but it did nothing to slow her narrative. She held her hands up as if holding a small object. "Grandpa was on the other side of the street taking a photo of her leaving church. One of her friends pointed out his action to grandma."

"Why would he be across the street taking a photo of his own wife?" This story made no sense. He only hoped it got better. Surely there could be no comparison of himself and a man crossing streets to photograph his wife. At least, he hoped not.

The aide, whose name tag identified her as Sheila, chuckled. "They hadn't met yet. Grandma was a widow and grandpa a long-time bachelor who attended the same church. Anyhow, when grandma saw him taking her photo, she marched right across the street and…"

"I know…" Jake interrupted. "She snatched the camera out of his hands." A similar incident had happened to him in France.

"No." Sheila shot Jake a confused look. "She invited him to lunch. They got to know each other and married not too long after."

Well, that hadn't turned out the way he thought it would. Too bad he didn't have that kind of luck. At the moment, he'd be fortunate if the helpful Sheila hit the road. "Great story," he enthused. "I appreciate the help, too. Don't let me cut into your break, though."

"No problem," she assured.

Being a few steps away from her, Gus stood and cupped his hands around his mouth, yelling to Jake. "Hey! What are you doing over there?"

Before Jake could say anything, Sheila did for him. "He's taking secret photos of his crush."

Geesh, that sounded creepy. Normally, his friend didn't always hear what the staff said. Gus often complained they mumbled or slurred their words. Unfortunately, the gleam in his eyes announced he'd heard Sheila's comment just fine. He rubbed his hands together. "Can't wait to tell Eunice."

"Don't you dare!" Jake darted in front of the courtyard doors before Gus could open them.

He huffed and grumbled to himself. "Party pooper. I remember when you used to be fun."

When he used to be fun. Jake had to wonder when that was. "I *am* fun," he practically growled the words.

Gus rolled his eyes, not impressed by the words or the actions.

Instead of moving on, Sheila kept an avid gaze on the two of them, obviously enjoying the show.

A garbled message sounded over the PA system, making no sense with its series of numbers and color, but it got Sheila moving quickly—one less person to witness Jake's humiliation.

He needed to prevent Gus from blabbing about a crush. "I've got an idea. How about we go into the courtyard and say I'm doing an article about the croquet tournament. Then I take photos of everyone whacking the ball or wielding a mallet or something."

It would give him the perfect excuse to take photos without lurking in the hall like a weirdo. All he needed was for his friend to play along. However, with Gus nothing was a sure bet.

"Huh?" Gus cupped a hand by his ear.

Jumping Jehoshaphat! He knew the man heard him. If Gus could hear Sheila, he could certainly hear Jake. No help for it, he tucked his phone into his pocket and pulled out his wallet and opened it. He withdrew a five-dollar bill.

Gus licked his lips.

If he was going to pay his friend off, he'd better win the money back during their weekly poker game, which wasn't a given since everyone cheated. He pushed back the five and pulled out a twenty instead. Gus snatched it from his fingers. "That sounds like a great plan. Let's do it!"

Chapter Eleven

KNOWING HE WOULD pay for this in more than a monetary form, Jake followed Gus into the courtyard. If their entrance hadn't garnered enough attention, Gus announced in an overloud voice, "Jake needs to take your photos for the Greener Pasture Gazette!"

They hadn't agreed exactly why he needed their photos. His original thought was something about an article—nothing concrete he could be tied to and questioned when it didn't appear. Herman raised his bushy eyebrows while his wife, Lola, tried to suppress a knowing smile without too much success. The object of his mission nodded her head in silent acknowledgment.

Eunice, still clutching the mallet, pointed it at Jake. "What newspaper?"

"You heard Gus. The Greener Pastures Gazette."

"Yeah, I heard." Her eyes narrowed as she lowered the mallet. "I came up with the name so I know all about it. I also happen to know the activity director shot down my plans for a newspaper when I suggested it. She claimed it was too much trouble."

Not good. Jake cut his eyes to Gus who refused to meet his gaze. Had the man forgotten Eunice wanted to start a newspaper and accidentally picked out the name she'd planned on using? Or had he just paid his friend to use him as the butt in another one of his practical jokes.

"She changed her mind. The paper is now a go. I'm here to take photos for the croquet tournament." Knowing that Eunice enjoyed being in the spotlight, he added, "Don't you want your photo taken?"

A derisive sniff served as an answer. Eunice glanced away and sighed. Just when Jake thought he'd escaped being pierced by her rapier tongue, her head snapped back to level a glare on him. "Soooo…" She lengthened the word. "The activity director suddenly changes her mind." She arched her eyebrows and firmed her lips together.

Jake gulped, aware that what some people would think was a simple sentence also worked as the opening volley. Too bad he had no ammunition. Eunice pointed her index finger at him. "It's because you're a man. That's why she's letting you do the newspaper. *My* newspaper."

"Ah…" Jake hesitated, wondering if he should confess to making the whole thing up or throw Gus under the bus. It would serve Gus right for his part in it. Still, she might not even believe him. "You're right. The newspaper would be too much trouble. The only reason she agreed is Katie would help me with it."

In the normal scheme of things, Eunice didn't give up easily. She usually got in a few more jabs, even if she was winning. The old saying about being gracious in victory and humble in defeat didn't apply. However today, the eyebrows lowered, and she managed a slight nod. "Well, that makes sense. I'm sure Katie would be a big help. Keep in mind, I'd like to work on the paper, too."

Jiminy Cricket. Not only did he have a mythical newspaper with his niece Katie helping, but Eunice wanted to work on it, too. This meant he'd now have to come up with a newspaper on his own. Run it a couple of weeks before letting it fade away, which might not be entirely possible if Eunice took a hand in it. "I'm sure you could write an article or two."

Hannah held up a hand and wiggled her fingers. "I'd like to write something, too. Writing has always been a hobby of mine. What do you need? Human interest, recipes, poetry, or mainly local news?"

If Hannah wrote something, it would only be natural if he went over it. His heart sped up a little at the prospect. Gus's blathering provided the perfect opportunity to catch the striking woman in a lie. He hesitated as he tried to remember what his role in this newspaper thing would be. He hadn't indicated anything other than he had permission to create a paper. Maybe he was the editor in chief. The thought pleased him because he could tell Eunice what to do—not that she would listen. Hannah kept her dark eyes on him awaiting his answer.

"Sounds great," Jake replied.

"You didn't tell me what you needed."

He hadn't. Jake flashed a wide grin as a form of apology. "Ha ha, you got me there. Tell you the truth, since this is our first edition, we need everything. Write what you feel, and I'll fit it in."

"Me, too?" Eunice inquired with a glimmer in her eye that boded no good.

"Of course. I trust you." His eyes turned upward at that whopper, certain lightning would strike him. To be fair, he trusted Eunice not to kill him and possibly warn him of anyone who might. What he didn't trust was her ability to resist poking at him any time she could. Disaster averted, he needed pictures.

Jake held up his phone. "How about some photos of our intrepid croquet players?"

The group broke apart and milled a little bit, uncertain what to do. It was the perfect time to take candid shots he hoped wouldn't be blurry. Most were backs or profiles with people moving to get out of a shot. Nothing that could be used to identify a person.

Lola grimaced. "By *intrepid*, I assume you mean not afraid to make fools of themselves."

"No, not at all." Jake should watch his words. His easy compliments were for those who didn't examine them too closely. Senior Sleuths paid a great deal of attention to everything. Even the smallest thing could be the needed item to close the case.

The sound of clapping meant Eunice was taking control. "C'mon. We need to be serious about this. I imagine this issue will come out before the tournament. You need to look fierce so we can scare the competition."

"Ha!" Lola snorted the word. "It's a game best known for being played by Victorian ladies in big hats. It's not exactly the roller derby. What would you have us do? Brandish the mallet over our heads in a threatening manner as we glower?"

"Good idea." Eunice picked up her abandoned mallet, took a batter's stance, and frowned in Jake's direction. "Ah, that's a good one." He snapped a couple knowing Eunice would want to pick from them. "Anyone else?"

Glances were exchanged before Gus picked up a croquet ball and tossed it with a jaunty grin. Obviously, he wasn't going for the fierce look. Herman held out his arm for Lola, who gripped a mallet in her free hand. Jake knew the former showgirl was self-conscious about her walker and made sure not to include it in the frame.

"Who's next?" Jake called out, trying not to make a point of who hadn't had their photo taken.

"Hannah's next," Eunice informed Jake while handing the woman a mallet. "Just look natural. Since no one knows you, they'll have no clue how good you are. Try for a smirk."

"Oh, I don't know." She made eye contact with each of the senior sleuths. "I don't even know if I'm going to stay here or not."

"Got anything better in the offing?" Gus asked. The man's plainspoken ways just skirted rudeness.

"Well, I…" She twirled the mallet an inch or two above the ground. Her gaze stayed on the mallet as if it were the most fascinating thing she had glimpsed in her life. Finally, she gave her head a shake. "I really don't."

"Why not move in today?" Gus held his hands palms up as if the idea was a no brainer. It was like the approach he had used on Jake. What the center didn't need was a con artist.

Afraid he'd get no photo, he fussed with his phone, pretending to adjust it while he snapped photos. Not the best, since at least one part of Hannah was always in motion. Hands wouldn't be that important for identification.

"Not today," Hannah sucked in her lips. "There's a lot to be done. It's not a matter of packing a bag and taking a cab."

Most of the sleuths murmured their understanding, except for Eunice. "The tournament is in two weeks. You'll need to make up your mind before then. Even though I'm sure you're a decent player, practice will be needed."

"Oh…" Hannah replied with a slight breathiness. Maybe Eunice's acerbic manner surprised her after an afternoon of being fawned over.

A few of the shots were okay, showing Hannah's face and in a few, she even smiled. All he needed to do was slip back to his room and upload the images.

"I'd better get going and start working on my articles." He pivoted toward the door before anyone answered, but a simple inquiry stopped him.

"I thought you were going to take *my* photo,"

Ah yes. Taking off without Hannah's picture might be on the peculiar side. "Sure. I'm glad you reminded me." After several pictures of the same pose since he held his finger down too long, he thanked Hannah and tried to exit again.

Gus pantomimed looking at his watch, and then flashed one open hand and an index finger on the other hand. They'd meet at six and be ready for when Lance arrived. The man overlooked the obvious fact that others could see him and may be curious about his actions. "I'll see you at dinner."

Maybe by that time, he'd have information on who Hannah *really* was. If he did, he hoped she wasn't around to hear it. As small-time hustlers went, she had a guileless smile and a fetching manner.

Chapter Twelve

IMAGES OF HOW Jake would wiggle information out of Lyre's sister with clever questions filled his mind as he strolled back to his room with hands in his pockets and a self-satisfied smile. The original purpose of the Senior Sleuths was to help Marcy with some of the details about older crimes. Seniors, like themselves, would know what passed for gossip forty years ago, what buildings had been torn down, and what streets renamed. Another purpose leaned more toward kindness. Too often, seniors were considered stuck in the past or of no use in the present. Marcy recognized they might not be able to break into a sprint, but the mental cogs still turned. Unlike the overwhelmed police force, they had buckets of time to brainstorm about forensic photographs and possible motivations. Four solved cases under their belt proved they were no slackers.

Jake's steps slowed as he remembered the last couple of cases. At first, everyone crowded around Marcy's table and worked as a team. The last couple of times, Herman and Lola would head out together or sometimes it was Gus and Eunice. Talk about being a fifth wheel. However, not this time. This time, he and Gus would drive the bus. The case required some decent clues along with a name or two. The notes sounded like Lorelei and Lyre weren't exactly tight. Still, the reason behind that could be a clue, too.

Somehow, he had to find a way to keep Gus from gabbing away.

While his good-natured rambling amused some, others dismissed him as a chatty old man. Not the image Jake hoped to portray. His phone vibrated underneath his hand. A call or possibly a message—he hadn't learned how to differentiate between the two. A quick check of the screen showed a message from Lance. His pace picked up as he maneuvered around residents with a friendly nod. No time to talk, Jake, the Sleuth, needed to be in his office to review the message. His room functioned as his office.

Once he reached his room, unlocked the door, and slid inside, he made sure to relock it. No reason to issue a visiting invitation to whoever might be walking by. Normally, that didn't happen, except for Gus.

Jake moved to the window for better light and pulled out his phone. After swiping right, using his security symbol, and tapping on the message icon, Lance's message popped open.

Can't make it tonight. Got the basket together. Will drop it off at the center. We can do it another night. If you promise to play it safe, maybe Herman could drive you.

A heavy sigh escaped his lips. Herman didn't drive at night. The few times they got caught out past sunset, the drive home spiked his blood pressure more than the case itself. Besides, if Herman drove, Lola would come. If Lola came, Eunice would have to tag along. For all he knew, they'd try to shoehorn Hannah into the sedan. There wouldn't be any room for himself. His brow furrowed as he considered his dilemma. A sleuthing visit to Lorelei as the Parrot Birthday Club guys required a vehicle to get them there.

Without Lance, they were stuck. In a bigger town, there might be a bus or a subway. Whatever bus service they had dwindled to a few routes that hit the major spots such as the mall, the courthouse, and the hospital. Odds didn't favor Lorelei living along one of those well-traveled routes.

The best he could do was check it out online. A familiar startup chime sounded as he booted up his computer. Jake busied himself with pulling out case notes as the laptop warmed up. Since it was a gift, he shouldn't complain, but it had to be one of the earlier, slower models. Like Eunice, he wanted to clap his hands to make it go faster, but he resisted the temptation. Placing the notes on the table, he pulled out a chair and sat.

Gus flipped through the sheaf of papers until he found Lorelei's address—4949 Doe Meadow Woods. It sounded poetic. It had to be one of those new neighborhoods that had popped up in the last thirty years. Contractors christened their creations with creative monikers that were often the exact opposite of the location. Even though Indiana sat six hundred miles from the nearest ocean, plenty of streets bore names reminiscent of beachy communities, including Sea Harbor, Sea Breeze, Seashell Court, and even Outer Banks Drive. A street called Serenity Woods had about a seventy percent chance of being an inner-city development that was far from serene.

Doe Meadow Woods was either part of the suburban sprawl around the university or a transitional area, formerly farmland, but now served as a connector to the next city over of Clarksville. Neither place was served by the bus line.

Before Herman's appearance with his oversized sedan, Gus and Jake undertook a bus experiment to see where they could go on their own. What they realized was the center's weekly shuttle trips serviced the same areas without the hardship of buying a bus pass. None of their crime-solving adventures were on bus routes. The problem with mass transportation was it didn't come when you needed it to and forget the fast getaway. The image of them all waiting at a bus stop clutching their passes with a bad guy on their trail caused him to grimace.

Maybe he could take a taxi. By this time, the Internet icon on his screen appeared. *About time,* he thought, as he pulled up his favorite search engine. His niece, Katie, insisted they had good service at the center. It tended to slow down when the various planned daytime activities ended and residents retired to their rooms to watch television, surf the web for cute animal videos, or stalk their relatives or other center members on social media.

A few clicks revealed the bus routes became even more limited after six p.m. A taxi it was, then. Jake shuddered. As a Midwesterner who almost always had a car, he had little experience with taxis, except for the time he hailed one when returning from an overseas tour of duty. The vehicle came complete with the lingering smell of vomit. Just the thought decades later made him doubt the wisdom of using a taxi. Gus would have a heyday at his expense if he knew of his fastidiousness. It looked like they weren't going tonight. Whoever was behind Lyre's disappearance would have another day of freedom. He glared at the computer as if it were somehow to blame.

Uploading Hannah's photo on the computer to use reverse image lookup wasn't as easy as it sounded. Jake first had to make himself an email account that wasted twenty minutes as he eyed the various questions with suspicion. Was Big Brother going to be reading his mail? Once he had the account, he had to share a photo with his email. Another five minutes gone. Still, this could be useful in the future.

Various sites advertised reverse image search for a price. One called *Tin Eye* didn't cost anything so he clicked on it. Before trusting it with his Hannah pic, he found an image of a well-known actress and uploaded it onto the site. His lips tipped up as he pushed the enter button, proud that he was able to do this on his own. The results came back immediately, naming the star and even where the photo was taken. Good deal.

Cheered by the result, Jake loaded Hannah's photo with a touch of apprehension. All the sleuths had welcomed Hannah with open arms. Even he enjoyed her ready wit and husky laugh. Unfortunately, her façade would be stripped away once he pushed the button. His mouth twisted to one side while considering the consequences. If the results came back with a police report attached to it, he'd have to say or do something.

His finger pressed down slowly on the mouse and clicked. A few seconds later, the information came back. No long stream of letters. Instead, just three words: *Image Not Found*. As if an apology, the site asserted it had searched over three million records.

He leaned back into his chair with a relieved sigh. At least this saved him from breaking the bad news. His eyes closed for a brief second as he considered the logical applications. Where did the site search? Did it include newspapers, websites, news shows, and privately released PR where it dug for information? If so, would the wife of a washed-out astronaut even be recognized? What he needed to do was find an astronaut's wife and put *her* in the search. He opened his eyes and wrinkled his nose at doing so. The prospect would put it right back where he was five minutes ago.

The squeak of the dietary cart meant dinner loomed near. Jake pushed up from the table with more energy than normal. This matter could wait. He needed to get to dinner and consult Gus about the loss of a ride. Nevertheless, Gus would immediately ask Herman so as not to lose his place in the sedan.

His eyes dropped to the glowing computer screen that featured ads along the edge for everything from stock images to ride services. *Wait a minute!* He leaned over the computer. Eunice had used such a service in the past. In her case, it billed her daughter's credit card. While it allowed Eunice the ability to get around, it also allowed the daughter to track her movements.

He had a credit card. It would take him a couple of minutes to sign up, but it wasn't like he'd lose his seat at the table. At least, he hoped not. Other residents might invite themselves over if Hannah still lingered at the center. Jake withdrew his wallet, sat, and rushed through the application. Not a professional on the keyboard, he misspelled his name, which he corrected. Then there was the address. Would a driver pick up someone from a convalescent/retirement home? He pursed his lips as he considered the matter.

Of course, they would. Since you were charged for the ride, the driver automatically got paid. As far as he knew there were no legal ramifications attached to picking up a person. Jake clicked on the submit button only to hear a small ding. Weird. He noticed a small envelope at the bottom of his screen. He had mail.

"Oh look. My first spam mail." He clicked on the envelope all the same. It opened and revealed a welcome letter from the ride service. "I got five dollars off my first ride. Now all I need is the basket of parrot goodies and a quiet Gus."

A lively knock sounded before a woman's voice called out. "You got a delivery! An odd one, too."

Jake hurried to the door and swung it open to two tan arms wrapped around a wicker basket crammed with parrot treats, bird toys, a party hat, and an oversized birthday card. A tuft of curly black hair topped the basket and two blue uniformed legs completed the image. Jazzy, the second shift aide, never skimped on giving her opinion.

He held out his arms. "I'll take that."

Once she delivered the basket, Jazzy gave him a thoughtful look. "You know you can't have a parrot in your room. The administration decided that when everyone wanted their own pet." She placed a hand on her chest. "No problem as long as you clean up after it. I won't tell, but it might be hard to keep quiet, especially if it talks."

Her wide wink made Jake grin. "I appreciate the offer. The truth is this is for a friend outside the home whose parrot has a birthday coming up."

"Huh?" Jazzy arched her eyebrows, drawing attention to her expressive eyes. "People are doing that now? My cat has never had a birthday party, and he's five years old. Snickers has been cheated out of catnip mice and tuna treats." She smirked and added, "Have fun at your parrot party."

"I will," Jake promised and gave the aide a friendly wave. As he deposited the basket on the bed, he realized he'd told Jazzy where he was going. One of the first rules of senior sleuthing was never leak out details of adventures. "Dang!"

Oh well, nothing would come of it. Why would a parrot birthday party be of any interest to anyone?

Chapter Thirteen

THE PARROT BASKET rested on the table as Jake scrolled through the icons on his cell phone. Since he was in his room alone, it didn't matter if he talked to himself. Out in the halls, doing the same would have plenty of people trying to answer while the staff would make a note of it in his file. "Too many stupid icons. I should get rid of some of them. Where's that ride app anyhow?"

He slid his finger across the screen and harrumphed. "Don't see it."

Finally, he found it under featured apps. "All right! Got it."

An index card contained a few questions that he needed to commit to memory. Nothing shouted *scam* as much as reading off a card. Personally, Lorelei might consider his reading off a card reader to be more of a novice move as opposed to that of a hardened criminal. Before they left, he needed time for a confab with Gus. The idea had him texting his friend that now would be a perfect time. He couldn't do it at supper since the other sleuths would be present and possibly Hannah.

Where are you?

He frowned at the phone in his hand. Did Gus even have his phone with him? Unlike the younger folks, his friend had decades of walking around not being at the beck and call of everyone using a digital device. He might not even have noticed he didn't have it with him. Jake huffed, and was patting his pockets to check the location of his room key when his phone vibrated. A glance confirmed it was Gus.

Bingo.

It was hard to know if his friend was shouting the word if involved in the game or it was some type of bizarre greeting like *you've got mail.* Of course, Gus would go with something shorter. The man hated to text. Then again, Gus texted the way he talked, often not making any sense initially.

Jake typed. *Huh?*

The game. You've played it before.

He knew what bingo was. Gus must be joshing with him. Before he could reply, another message showed on his phone.

We managed to extract Hannah from the greedy claws of Lola and Herman. We're trying to sell her on Greener Pastures. BTW, Gus asked me to text since he's so slow at it. This is Eunice.

Now it made sense. So much for meeting Gus before they took off on the parrot club mission. He might as well practice his questions. At least he'd sound more natural as opposed to sounding scripted.

Two hours later, after a rushed dinner of swiss steak and mashed potatoes, Jake cradled the large parrot basket as he waited in the hallway close to Gus's room. Technically, his friend wasn't allowed to venture out on his own. His family worried about him getting into trouble. Whenever he did leave to put in some footwork for a case, Gus had to be creative about his exit. They usually left by the newest wing that featured modest apartments with a strip of a kitchen, a postage stamp living room, and a full bath and bedroom for twice the price Jake paid for his studio-style room. Not this time, though.

Getting lazy was the fastest way of getting caught. An overheard conversation between an aide and a custodian revealed the center featured a single door that had neither camera nor alarm—perfect for a quick smoke. They'd have to make sure no smokers saw them leave. If they were spotted, his excuse would be they were walking around the grounds. Many residents strolled around outdoors to catch a bit of fresh air and enjoy nature.

After waiting for him a good ten minutes, Gus came up behind Jake. "I'm here!"

His loud declaration surprised Jake, making him jump. His eyes shifted to his friend, then back to Gus's room.

"I wasn't in my room." He gave his head a shake. "We were all saying goodbye to Hannah. Everyone, except you." Reproach filled the last two words.

"Didn't know I was supposed to be there."

"It's okay," Gus assured with a grin. "I explained that you like to play hard to get."

"Geesh!" He shot one hand through his dark hair. "We need to get going. I'll send a message for our ride, but it may arrive before we get outside. Where did you say you were going?"

Since Eunice and Gus had been keeping company for the last couple of months, they spent their evenings together. Lola and Herman had moved to an extra-large suite once they married and spent their evenings tucked away, too.

It wasn't like Gus could disappear for a few hours without an explanation. Eunice could smell a lie, which made her a valuable member of the Senior Sleuths. This same talent made it hard to run anything past her. Jake pulled out his phone, pulled up the app, and hit submit since he had the address preprogrammed.

Gus cleared his throat and said, "No problem. I told Eunice I was going to buy her a present."

"Why?"

"Good boyfriends do that. They shower their lady love with gifts to show their affection."

Jake snorted, "You hear that on a commercial?"

"Nope. Eunice told me."

"Figures." Jake twisted his lips as if he'd bit into something bitter. Before his friend could see it, he smoothed his features into a non-committal expression. No reason for him to make snarky comments since he remained firmly unattached. A box of candy or a thoughtful gift didn't require major financial outlay. If it kept the tumultuous water of love smooth, it was well worth it. He blew out a long breath as he considered his lack of gift-giving to the fairer sex. As a military pilot, he had earned points gifting foreign women with chocolate bars and cigarettes while stationed abroad. While the women were appreciative, it couldn't be called a gift since it came in his soldier rations.

Bachelors bore nicknames such as *lucky dog* or *swinging single*. Women didn't have such time-honored labels for remaining single. It may have taken a few years to figure it out, but he decided unattached males made these names up to add to the myth of the single guy. They didn't want to fess up to being lonely and somehow responsible for their unattached status. Enough of this reflection on his current marital state—a cold case waited to be solved.

Jake placed a finger to his lips and motioned for Gus to follow.

They walked without talking in an effort not to catch the eye of a staff member or resident who might hope to draw them into a conversation. After a few turns, they finally reached a short hall used mainly for storage. Fewer lights illuminated the area, making it shadowy. There was no reason for lights if no one used the hall except for the occasional custodian or smoker.

Before pushing the exit door open, Jake shot a furtive glance over his shoulder. Spotting no one, he inhaled and pushed the door open, hoping no smokers had slipped out for a quick cigarette. Stale cigarette smoke, along with a sweetish odor of a flavored slender cigar, hung like a curtain outside the door. Fortunately, no people lingered nearby. "Okay," Jake spoke, inhaling the stale smoke at the same time.

Hand movements served as he gestured for Gus to follow him around the wing to reach the front entrance where the ride would be waiting. Windows showed as lighted rectangles on the ground as they skirted the building. Muffled conversations and television shows merged with the evening air. A woman stood inside a window with her hands braced on the curtains as if to close them when she must have spotted their silhouettes.

A screech penetrated the air along with the words, "Peeping Toms!"

Jake and Gus broke into a run without the need to consult one another. Action served better than overthinking the situation. The long front porch crowded with chairs functioned as their sanctuary as the two stumbled onto the porch and collapsed into nearby chairs. Jake placed the basket beside his chair, half-hidden in the shadows. The double doors opened.

Jake nodded in Gus's direction and said in a loud voice, "So, how about the Reds? They've had a pretty good year."

Gus remained silent, making Jake think he didn't understand they were pretending to be on the porch the entire time talking sports. An aide with a pinched expression stomped out onto the porch, clutching a walkie talkie in one hand while fisting her free hand. Her head cut to the right, then left, and after spotting Gus and Jake, she marched over to them. Gus chose that moment to announce, "I've always been a Yankees fan."

The aide gave them a glassy glare and asked in a sharp tone, "You all see anyone lurking about the building?"

Jake answered first. "Nope. Were you expecting someone?"

Instead of answering, the woman exhaled audibly.

Gus's eyebrows shot up, indicating his intention to embellish the story some. "We've been here for the last twenty minutes or so. It's hard to tell the time when you're outside and there isn't a clock about. What we need is a clock outside. I'd hate to miss Matlock."

A walkie talkie in the aide's hand crackled to life. "Anything?"

"Nothing." The woman walked away from Jake and Gus but continued to use an overloud voice people often use with digital devices as if sheer volume would penetrate the airwaves. "Couple of old dudes yakking on the front porch. I doubt they've moved in the last decade. Said they didn't see anything." The aide added a dismissive sniff as if their reply or their eyesight could be faulty or possibly both.

A small car with its headlights on slid into the parking lot and moved slowly toward the entrance. Gus leaned in Jake's direction. "I think that's our ride."

"I know." Jake tamped down his anxiety about the possibility of the driver leaving without his fare. His gaze shifted to the aide, who stood near the door complaining about the resident who had sounded the alarm. "We need Miss Helpful to go inside."

"I wouldn't call her helpful."

"I'm being sarcastic," Jake pointed out as his phone vibrated in his pocket. He retrieved his cell and peered at it in the low light. "It's our ride."

"Tell him you'll be right out," Gus instructed and wiggled his fingers, which must mean texting.

Weird. If it wasn't bad enough that he was asking a stranger to drive him around, now he was texting the driver as if they knew each other. He glanced at the phone. "He gave me the thumbs-up sign."

"She's gone," Gus reported as he stood. "Let's hit it."

Jake gathered up his basket and hurried after Gus. It almost sounded like Gus thought he was in charge. At least the driver knew where to go.

About twenty minutes later, after a series of turns on unfamiliar streets and subdivisions with names such as Deer Hollow, Deer Park, Doe Haven, they finally arrived at Doe Meadow Woods. The driver stopped in front of a modest ranch with a stone and vinyl façade. The fenced front yard consisted of patchy grass with a couple of pots of mums turning brown. An abandoned pink tricycle indicated a child inside.

Jake thanked the driver, mentioned he'd need a ride back, and grabbed the basket. His friend climbed out the other door. Together, they met at the front gate as the car zoomed away. "He was supposed to wait."

"It doesn't work that way," Gus informed him with a grin. "Just as well. I think I saw our driver on that show where they show America's most wanted."

"They canceled that show a long time ago."

"It doesn't mean they aren't still wanted. Maybe our next ride will be some young beauty working her way through college."

"Great. Let me talk. I've worked out questions while you've been playing bingo."

A snort greeted his announcement. "You can thank me later. I was busy trying to convince Hannah to join our little community."

It didn't feel like the right time to explain Hannah wasn't who she pretended to be, so Jake simply said, "Thanks. Keep in mind, we didn't call ahead. So, there's a possibility that Lorelei could react in a hostile manner."

Gus chuckled and slapped Jake on the back. "I'll let you handle it, then. You always seem to have one or two females mad at you."

Chapter Fourteen

THE PORCH LIGHT cast a circle of illumination on the cement porch. It spotlighted another withered plant, causing Jake to shake his head. Apparently, Lorelei didn't have a green thumb. He only hoped the parrot fared better or this was going to be a very short visit. Even though he needed the mental stimulation and adventure the cold cases provided, there existed in every case a moment when he wondered what in the world he was doing. This was it. Stiff upper lip and all that, he reminded himself, inhaled deeply, and knocked on the door.

A young voice called out, "I'll get it!"

The door swung open, revealing a gap-toothed preschool girl with a smear of jelly across her face. She grinned and pointed to the basket. "Is that for me?"

"Only if you're a parrot." Jake returned her smile while he mentally improvised his speech. He had no clue he'd be addressing a much younger female.

A giggle sounded as she backed up a step to point behind her where a large African Grey Parrot sat. "Shut Up is a parrot. His real name is Parroty. It means something like a copy, but not quite. Mommy always calls him Shut Up.

On cue, the parrot swiveled its head to stare in their direction and screeched, "Shut up. Shut up. Shut up. Didn't you hear me the first time?"

Well, it certainly explained the name. Jake heard several stories of talking birds who chose to imitate whatever you didn't want them to say, including a parrot owned by a preacher that swore. A woman with wet hair strolled into the room, buttoning her shirt. "Ellie, who was at the…" Her inquiry stopped when she spotted Jake and Gus inside and asked in a tight voice, "Who are you?"

Jake knew he had to answer fast since her eyes were roaming the room, possibly searching for her cell phone to call 911 or any object she could use as a weapon. "Hello. I'm Jake. This is my partner, Gus. We are with the Parrot Birthday Club. Our job is to deliver delightful, birthday baskets created with your bird in mind to celebrate its birthday or the day of their pet union."

"Pet union?" she echoed the words with a furrowed brow.

Maybe that wasn't the best choice of words—he had also considered *anniversary*. "The day you were united with your parrot."

Gus gave a little wave as if somehow people could fail to see him. "It's like the day you and your parrot first fell in love."

That didn't sound any better than the pet union phrase. Lorelei must have thought so, too because she grimaced. "I am so *not* in love with that parrot."

An avian voice called out, "Love you, too!"

So far, so good, Jake considered, and held out the basket. "Here's the basket you ordered." He nodded in the bird's direction. "That must be the lucky bird unless you have another one."

Instead of taking the basket, Lorelei's eyes narrowed, and she stepped away from it. "I'm not paying you for something I didn't order. I know how these scams work. My sister was an investigative reporter so I know this stuff. You better leave before I call the police, and you can take your basket with you."

Ellie dashed to her mother and tugged on her shirt. "Please, Momma, it's a gift for Shut Up."

Hearing his name, the parrot started again. "Shut up. Shut up. Why won't you do what I say?"

Jake kept his gaze on Lorelei, knowing he'd have to make it okay to take the basket. "You prepaid for the basket. I think it was two years ago." He turned to nod in Gus's direction. "Two years, huh?"

Gus bobbed his head vigorously. "That's right. We tried to deliver it last year, but we had some issues with the address. The man at the apartment insisted we had the wrong place. Because we were late, we threw in some extra quality parrot supplies."

All he wanted his friend to do was agree, not give some long speech. He nodded at the woman, "You're Lyre McGovey, aren't you?"

"No." She glared at the two. "You're not one of those tabloid reporters here to try to do some scandalous story where you make up most of it."

This was not going the way he expected. He hadn't scripted this type of interaction. "Ah, can I put the basket down? It's heavy."

The parrot broke in with, "He's not heavy, he's my brother!"

Lorelei snorted, then motioned for Jake to put the basket down. After an awkward silent minute, she said, "I'm not Lyre. Can't you guys even remember what she looked like?"

Talk about a hole in their plan. It never occurred to him he'd be expected to identify Lyre or at least know when someone wasn't her. Shut Up chirped, adding to the conversation. "Remember! Must remember! Lighthouse 4106."

A possibility coalesced in Jake's mind. The parrot was certainly chatty and tended to respond to familiar words in conversation. It wasn't exactly like they were carrying on a conversation, but he interrupted quite a bit, obviously starved for attention. What if the bird heard something before his owner vanished? So far, the bird hadn't screamed or shouted *help me*, which must mean he didn't witness an abduction. Lyre wasn't taken from her home or the woman had cooperated and left on her own. If only he could work his way closer to the cage, but two strange old guys showing up with a basket of bird goodies naturally didn't put the woman at ease.

Gus coughed, then spoke. "Well, you see..."

Oh no. Jake rolled his eyes, but outside of covering his friend's mouth with his hand, he didn't know what else to do. Maybe whatever he said would be harmless enough.

"You see," Gus repeated himself, "when you get as old as I am, all the young, pretty girls look pretty much the same."

A derisive snort meant the blatant flattery had missed its mark. "Ah, yeah," Lorelei started, "I'm not buying it."

The doddering old man act served his friend well. Most people tried to make sense of his nonsense. Although he had a feeling Lorelei would cut it short, Ellie abandoned her hold on her mother's shirt and padded over to poke at the basket. "Shut Up got a lot of nice stuff. Is there anything for me?"

"Ah, no," Jake admitted. "I'm sure you could have the basket and the birthday signage. A parrot wouldn't have much use for it." He didn't expect either item to be much of a hit. Still, Ellie smiled at him.

"Would you like to meet Shut Up?"

Out of the mouth of a child came his perfect opportunity. "I'd love to meet him."

Jake listened to judge where Gus was in his routine. It sounded like he'd reached when he was in the war. At best, he had five minutes before a halt would be called on the rambling narrative. Sure, people tended not to give an old man the bum's rush, especially when the individual was also a veteran. Everyone had a breaking point and five minutes would be more than most would listen without inventing an urgent matter that needed immediate attention.

Jake ambled after Ellie, trying not to draw attention to himself. The parrot flapped his wings and resettled on his perch as they approached. The closer he came to the bird, the more its eyes glittered with intelligence, but it quashed that idea by saying, "Look what the cat dragged in!"

"Television," Ellie explained. "He watches a lot of television. Most of the time it keeps him quiet, but now and then he picks up new phrases."

"Very clever. He sounds like he knows a lot of words. Let me try something." His plan was to give the bird a bunch of words to see how he'd respond. "Hello."

"Goodbye!"

Classic. Maybe Shut Up was a Beatles fan.

"Cheesecake." Jake suggested the word, not taking time to think of something logical.

"Kansas."

How did that relate? Did he mean the state?

"Remember." Jake enunciated the word clearly since it was the only one, he cared about.

"Lighthouse!" Shut Up responded immediately.

Ellie nudged him. "Usually he says 4106, too. I think you're making him nervous." She pointed to the bird's feet scooting back and forth across the perch.

"Nonsense. Birds like me. Don't ya?" He put out his index finger to rub it over the feathers the way he used to with his own parakeet decades ago. Ol' Petey loved a little massage on his back.

"Ouch!" Jake jerked back his hand. "Your bird bit me."

"He does that." Ellie shrugged. "Mommy says he has no manners. Rude bird."

"Oh, that's it!" Lorelei shouted. "I don't know who you are. I tried to be nice, but you need to leave now. Both of you!"

Jake pulled out a cloth handkerchief and wrapped his bleeding finger. "Will do." He caught Gus's eye and headed for the door.

Not taking any chances, Lorelei followed them outside wagging her index finger. "Don't waste your time on suing me because the parrot bit you. Since I don't have any money, you wouldn't get anything from me. It doesn't have rabies, so you're fine. I only took that stupid parrot because Lyre thinks the world of him."

She stomped one foot on the porch. "Get out of here!"

The night had darkened a little more, making it hard to discern the path. Fortunately, he and Gus got out of the front yard and past a neighbor's house without incident, and they slowed to a walk. Laughter bubbled out of Gus. He slapped his hand against his leg and snorted.

"Good Golly! You certainly got her heated up." He clicked his tongue. "You and women. Somehow you know what to do to upset them."

"I'm sure you had your part in the fiasco, too. At least *you* weren't bit."

"True." Gus agreed with a little too much glee. "When are we going to call for a ride?"

Yeah, a ride, that's what was missing in this scenario. They needed a getaway car. At this point, he'd settle for a bus. Dogs barked in the not too far distance and a door slammed. A low throated hum of a muscle car purred in the background. Most individuals who owned such a car tended to drive fast and roar up to intersections. Oddly, the car in question moved slowly.

A backward glance revealed a dark silhouette without even a color to identify the vehicle, and a trickle of unease nudged him. Rather than mention it, Jake decided as unofficial leader to choose their next move. "Let's try to find a public place. I'd prefer not to do any more running tonight in case we're mistaken for robbers casing a house."

"Yeah." Gus cleared his throat. "Remember, I also have to get Eunice a present."

"Uh-huh." Jake rubbed his forehead where a headache throbbed. "Present. Yeah. Maybe we can get the driver not to leave us this time."

Chapter Fifteen

THE PORCH LIGHTS of Greener Pastures silhouetted a woman standing on the front sidewalk. Jake wondered who it might be and if she were waiting for her own ride or hoped to stargaze. With all the illumination from the center, the nearby neighborhood, and the highway, she'd be lucky to spot the moon, let alone the constellations. His friend, Gus, stiffened up next to him and muttered something under his breath.

"What?" Jake asked, almost certain the remark hadn't been meant for his ears.

Gus elbowed Jake as a response. "You'd better be right about Eunice being a practical woman as opposed to a sentimental one."

"There's nothing soft or dewy-eyed about her. I'm sure she'll appreciate the soap and hand lotion you got her. It's stuff she needed anyhow. Not sure why you didn't get the deodorant since it was the same scent."

The female driver braked hard and turned to address her passengers. "He probably didn't get the deodorant because his instinct for self-preservation interfered." She singled out Jake by pointing. "Where in the world did you get off thinking women want soap and hand lotion? You must not be married."

"Divorced," Jake mumbled, wilting a little under the words. He tried to avoid talking about his short-lived marriage.

"Figures." The woman huffed and angled her head to the porch. "I assume that's your lady love waiting."

Gus gulped, then managed a whispery, "Yes."

"You're in luck." The corner of her lips lifted in a knowing smile. "I happen to have a smart man at home. When I take off to drive folks around, he makes sure I know how special I am. Tonight, he gave me a small box of chocolates. Haven't opened it yet, but I'd be willing to give it to you for a nice tip and a good review."

She arched her eyebrows. "I'd count it as a favor if you didn't mention all the fast driving and rapid turns." A heavy sigh escaped her. "I have a good man now, but I made the mistake of falling for a crazy possessive nutjob. Left him ten months ago, only he's not having it. I thought he was following me. He does that sometimes."

If some mentally unstable old boyfriend tended to follow her, then it might be best not to drive people around. It made Jake speculate what would happen if the boyfriend caught them. It did explain the driving. "Are you sure it was your ex?"

Her shoulders went up in a shrug. "Hard to see in the dark. Can't say I recognize the car. There's nothing to stop him from renting a car or even borrowing one. Had to be him unless you had someone chasing you?"

The woman laughed at her own remark as if the possibility was preposterous. If he chose to tell her he'd been in a car chase more than once, that would stop her laughter. Then again, she just might chuckle some more, convinced that he'd made it up. Instead, he asked, "Do you think it could have been someone unrelated who just tailgated a bit too hard and you overreacted?"

Silence greeted the question. Then their driver shrugged again. "Maybe. Remember, I stopped at the drug store and didn't charge you extra. If I'd known you were shopping for his sweetie, I'd have suggested something a little more upscale. All the same, remember I gave up my special chocolate. A good review and a big tip is fair."

More than fair in Jake's opinion since he got stuck with paying it.

"It's a deal!" Gus nudged Jake. "Remember—good review and a big tip. I'll show you how to work the app if you can't figure it out."

The inference that he couldn't operate a stupid app stung. "I can do it."

Gus accepted the candy with a hearty thank you, and they both bid the driver goodbye. The plastic bag rattled as the contents tumbled inside. When they reached the toe-tapping woman, it didn't surprise Jake that it was Eunice.

"Where have you two been?"

Any mention of sleuthing without her wouldn't please. Not being his problem, Jake decided to keep his mouth closed. Gus stepped forward with a grin and rattled his sack. "I've been shopping for you, my dear."

She clapped her hands together. "Oh goody! Let me see."

The possibility that Eunice might not love the hand lotion and soap had Jake side-stepping the couple to reach the door until the woman in question pivoted and speared him with a question. "Where are *you* going? While the two of you have been shopping, the rest of us have been working on the cold case. Hannah came up with something great on the torso before she left. Lola, Herman, and I did an Internet search and found out it was doable."

"Hannah?" His voice, tight with apprehension, went up on the word. His world wouldn't change being outed as a sleuth, except it might grow a bit duller. Lance and Marcy could lose their jobs. "Didn't you think about the consequences? You kept quiet this long about the Sleuths, why yak about it now?"

"Don't get your shorts in a wad." She waved off his concern with a hand gesture. "I'm no dummy. We didn't mention anything about a cold case. Instead, we talked about something we saw on television and how they couldn't identify the body because of its lack of head and hands. Hannah came up with a great way the body could still be identified even after being in the water for so long."

"How?" This could be a real game-changer for the case. It would make the difference between finding justice for Lyre or simply finding out the torso wasn't hers. Jake rocked forward on his toes expectantly while Eunice rooted through the bag.

"Chocolates!" she cooed. "The expensive kind, too."

"Nothing is too good for my baby."

"Ah. You really know the way to a girl's heart." Eunice pecked her beau on the cheek and beamed at him. After a few seconds, she said, "Let's see what other wonderful presents you got me."

Let's not, Jake thought. Apart from ripping the bag out of her hand, he couldn't do much to prevent it. As far as not being soft-hearted and sappy, Jake erred on that, too. Who would have thought of asking women for clues about a gift for Eunice? Certainly not him and apparently not Gus, either.

The bag crinkled as Eunice delved into it as if it were St. Nick's bag of treasures and slowly pulled out the soap. Unlike deodorant soaps enclosed in paper wrappers, this one came in a box with advertising that declared it was *English Lavender*.

Eunice's brows went down, and she opened the box and shook

it, causing a light purple bar to slide out. "It's soap."

Even though the box and the bar trumpeted the fact, Eunice still seemed confused. "I thought it would be something else. That's why I opened the box."

Jake sucked in his lips, aware he'd stepped into it now. Many words could apply to Eunice, including sly, smart, acerbic, and even creative. The woman wasn't above gossiping, manipulating, and at times outright lying if it served her purpose. What he had never witnessed was the hurt that was in her eyes now.

A tear slid down her face as she turned to face her sweetie. "Do you think I need to take a bath? Do I smell bad?"

Even before Gus spoke, Jake winced, guessing the possible outcome. His friend was quick to console his love with his own personal flattery. "I love the way you smell, especially the combination of Tabu dusting powder and cough drops. It's so you and so unique. Jake suggested the bath soap, calling it a practical gift for a practical woman."

Talk about a cue exit stage left, this was his. Before he could, something hit his arm. Jake glanced down to see the bag twirling for another hit. It still contained the lotion and possibly the soap since he lost track of what happened to it. Gus stood behind the angry female with an apologetic expression but doing nothing.

The bag hit him again, not as hard, though. It was more of a statement than an intent to hurt. "Don't give my boyfriend any more gift suggestions. He can do just fine on his own."

Truth was, he couldn't. Gus may have thrown him under the bus, but then again, maybe he did it himself. Why did he go suggesting what Eunice would like since he didn't excel at buying gifts for women or long-term romantic relationships? Jake held his hands up. "I won't make any more gift suggestions if you tell me what great information Hannah came up with."

The bag never reached him. Eunice pulled it back with a snap as her eyes lit up with the change of subject. "That Hannah knows a lot." She turned in the direction of the chairs. "Might as well sit since we dug up some possibilities and more questions."

The metal on cement groaning occurred as they arranged the chairs in a circle and took their seats. "That Hannah," she started, and then stopped and shook her head. "Not sure if I want her to be in the Senior Sleuths since she knows more than me. Weird, when you think about it—her boss being a private eye and all. I figured all they did was find lost people, take photos of cheating partners, occasionally check out date backgrounds to see if they're lying, and insurance work. Hannah knows a great deal about murder."

This didn't sound good. While he wasn't thrilled with the small-time con artist background he'd spun for the mysterious Hannah, the thought that she could be killer or kin to a killer appealed even less. Jake needed to find out more. "What made you think she knows about murder?"

"Well," Eunice made sure to make eye contact as she continued. "We told her the story about the torso not being identified because it had been in the water too long. She went on to tell us that DNA could be identified on clothes that had been washed or even in the water for a week. Sometimes, if bones are all you got, then a mitochondrial DNA test can be run. You get the mitochondrial DNA from the bone marrow. It's based on the X chromosome and can only be found in female relatives. Lyre would have to have a female relative for comparison purposes. We couldn't tell her about Lorelei, but we thought it all the same. We waited for her to leave to discuss the situation. We concluded someone didn't try too hard to identify the body. Do we even have photos? Did the sister identify the body? Maybe we should go talk to the sister."

That one Jake *could* answer. "It's not a good time to talk to the sister."

"Why?" Eunice inquired with a perplexed look. "It seems like the most logical thing to do."

Jake had thought the same. Still, he knew when to make himself scarce as he eased out of his chair. "I just remembered something I need to do."

Sometimes, he and Eunice didn't get along well. Make that *most* of the time. The one thing he could say about her was she had a sharp mind and made use of all the tools at her disposal, like how she mined Hannah for information, and then checked on the information online for its credibility. He'd stand a better chance finding out more about Hannah by letting Eunice loose on it. All in all, the fact the body wasn't identified and the case went immediately cold did make him wonder. His hand was on the door when he heard Eunice growl, "You did what?"

It sounded like the perfect time to go to his room and reflect on all this information.

Chapter Sixteen

AFTER SO MUCH running—although actual athletes would generously refer to it as *fast walking*—Jake reached for the pain reliever tablets. He'd take two and hit the shower. A hearty laugh sounded outside his door. It could turn out to be staff sharing personal stories, and he was too tired to investigate anyway. Instead, he turned on the radio to an easy listening station and made sure to lock his door.

In a place as big as Greener Pastures, a person had to carve out a signal that let passers-by know he was done for the night. Not that it would discourage Gus. He'd only claim he didn't hear the sleep station playing that Jake used as white noise. When Gus came up with an idea, he assumed whenever he thought of it was the best time to share.

Ten minutes later, Jake stretched out in his bed and stared upward at the ceiling, not really seeing it. The events of his Parrot Birthday Club fiasco played out on the screen of his mind. He couldn't say he got a lot from the visit, except that a tabloid journalist had been bugging Lorelei for information about her sister. Jake stretched his arms, hooked his fingers behind his head, and mulled over the situation. What little he knew about tabloid journalism was that they never actually interview people for facts. Usually, speculation served them well enough, along with Photoshopping photos to put people together who never were.

Jake jerked into a sitting position. It was a clue! Not a great one, but a clue all the same. Now all he needed to do was ask Lorelei if any of the press folks carried credentials. He sighed and flopped back onto his mattress. Devils had a better chance of ice skating than he had of getting back into that house. Even if Lorelei forgot about tonight and mistook him for a kindly old man, it didn't mean she'd say anything more than what she already had.

A sliver of light showed at the door bottom. It provided enough illumination to view his hand as he held up one finger. "People are coming around looking for information about Lyre. Possibly not press."

His middle finger joined his index finger. "Lorelei took the parrot while not being a fan as evidenced by his name, Shut Up. Her sole reason was that her sister loved the parrot."

Didn't Lance mention the two sisters weren't on good terms? As hard as he tried to remember, too much stuff tumbled around his head. Everything from Eunice being sentimental to wondering how Hannah knew about mitochondrial DNA scanning. Plus, their second driver made him a wee bit anxious. Sure, Gus thought he spotted their initial male driver on a reality crime show years ago. All those mug shots featured frowning men, usually with a scraggly beard. With certain age groups, that tended to be the preferred look.

No, the second driver had worried him when she made all those rapid turns after their drugstore stop. Her eyes stay glued to her rearview mirror for a long while. Nonetheless, she stayed in good spirits, even teasing Gus at the end. She'd made a point of emphasizing she had a good man, as opposed to her previous boyfriend, who may or may not have been following them. It also served as the basis for her Spy 101 driving. Still, her comment about someone following the two of them—that she laughed off—lodged somewhere in the back of his brain. What if someone had followed them? The better question would be, why?

"Ah!" Jake pounded his pillow. "I'm not going to get any sleep."

He sat up and dropped his bare feet to the floor. He'd read once in a magazine when you couldn't get to sleep, the best thing was to get out of bed and do something else until you were sleepy. He might as well write down what he did find, even though it wasn't much. He flipped on his bedside light and made his way to the table, where he turned on the overhead light.

At the table, he wrote down his two thoughts, staring at the two thin lines on the paper. Normally, the Sleuths did a better job as a team, coming up with clues. Most of the Sleuths had engaged in a song and dance routine to convince Hannah to move in. That meant he'd keep running into the woman, knowing that even her name wasn't her own. Eunice was all gaga over the mitochondrial DNA testing. If Hannah knew about it, then the police would, too. Why hadn't it been done already? Time to boot up the computer.

Jake pushed up from his chair to locate a snack. Since he normally took all his meals in the dining room, there wasn't much in his fridge besides condiments. The small freezer boasted a pot pie and half a loaf of bread. Toast functioned as an option, considering he also had butter and jam.

Snack assembled, he carried it to the table. Jake typed in *mitochondrial DNA testing* after making a few mistakes with the spelling. To his surprise, the search engine brought him all kinds of results. It *was* a thing. He took a bite out of his toast and chewed. At least

Hannah hadn't been lying about that. The sites included do it yourself kits from those family tree places. A basic kit was under a hundred dollars or so the site promised. It might be more like two hundred after various charges were tacked on.

The question was why wasn't a test performed that could easily identify the body? He flipped open the case file and scanned the pages. The majority were articles Lyre had written. Copies of the legal documentation of the court case, along with police notes, were included in the file. Jake picked up a photo of the missing journalist and regarded her unsmiling expression. Nope, not the type of woman to smile on cue. He had the feeling she also wouldn't be ordered around and trusted no one. At one point, he thought the parrot had a clue.

While the bird had a wide vocabulary, he never mentioned if Lyre had been abducted. Instead, he squawked *shut up, I love you, Lighthouse*, and a number. He scratched his head trying to remember the number. Was it 14? No, that wasn't right. He hadn't considered it important at the time. It still might not be. Jake knew it had a four and a one. The only other combination was 41. He grinned, knowing he nailed it, only there were two other numbers. What were they?

Jake wrote the numbers *four* and *one* in the center of the page. He also wrote out the numbers zero to nine and kept trying them in different combinations. He shot a hand through his hair. None of the numbers looked right. Wait a minute! He had only *heard* the numbers.

"Four one zero—that's it! Just one more number." He kept adding on numbers until he came to 4106. That had to be it! The parrot kept saying *remember lighthouse 4106*. Maybe Gus would know what it meant. He slipped on his shoes and belted his robe. Surely it wasn't too late to check if his friend had picked up any other clues.

As he turned to leave his room, he picked up his notepad and his room key. Sadly, a few of the residents who were not members of the Senior Sleuths liked to investigate other residents' rooms, which he didn't appreciate. Soft instrumental music still played in the hallway as he stepped out of his room. He'd heard some countries played classical music in prisons to keep the inmates calm. Not sure why they played it here. He shook his head, imagining the residents rioting and turned the key in the door lock. No reason for everyone to know his business.

On his way to find his fellow parrot party guy, he bumped into Herman and Lola. "Hello!" Jake nodded to them both. "Surprised to see you two out this late."

Lola shot him an amused look. "You never know what we might be up to. We find strolling the halls late in the evening can be quite the information gathering mission." A smug expression crossed her face, making Jake curious about what activities they'd espied on their rounds. "Where are you off to in such a hurry?"

Ahh, this would be difficult. He couldn't mention his recent adventure as a Parrot Birthday Club representative. "I needed to talk to Gus, um, about something. Yeah, I need to talk to him about something."

"Oh really?" Herman intoned in his baritone voice. His shaggy eyebrows did a bit of a dance of their own as if doing Morse code, which Jake couldn't remember. Was he trying to convey a message?

Jake held up his hand in parting. "Have a nice walk."

Fuchsia-colored nails stood out on Jake's plaid housecoat. He glanced down at Lola's hand and up to her knowing look as she spoke. "You wouldn't be going to see Gus about a parrot?"

How did she know? Jake sought Herman's face for confirmation, and the man gave a little nod. *Great.* Why did he ever think Gus could keep a secret? "Not sure why I thought I could trust Gus to keep his big mouth shut."

"That's a little hard," Lola added, giving his arm a squeeze before dropping her hand. "Consider that Gus is a man in love. It would be difficult to hide something from his beloved."

"Especially when that beloved is Eunice," he grumbled more to himself than anyone else.

His friends chuckled, meaning they heard. Herman moved closer and nudged Jake. "I'm not sure how much he told Eunice. I deduced most of it since the two of you vanished together. Didn't buy the story that you were helping pick out a gift. Tell you what, why don't we gather up all the sleuths and come back to our suite? We can have a midnight brainstorming session. It will be like we're..." He paused, rolling his eyes upward as he tried to think of an appropriate age. "...fifty-nine, again."

Chapter Seventeen

THE SMELL OF microwave popcorn permeated the room as Herman handed out plastic bowls brimming with the snack. Lola called out from her position at the kitchenette counter. "Anyone in the mood for decaf?"

Decaf wouldn't cut it. That much Jake knew since the case consisted of about ninety-nine percent of the unknown and unexplained. As for the known one percent, it didn't add up to a hill of beans. "Got any regular coffee? This will take a while."

"You got it," Lola answered cheerfully as she used the kitchen counters in the small area to help balance herself instead of her walker. The vivacious former showgirl added color to the small group as well as straight talk when it was needed, which turned out to be more of a daily thing as opposed to once in a blue moon.

Herman had rounded up the other sleuths while Jake returned to his room in search of the reports. With the upcoming croquet tournament and Hannah's visit, no one had had as much of a chance to deep dive into the case as he did. Brainstorming with the entire group might shake loose ideas he'd never considered. Even though he probably never mentioned it, Jake appreciated the input of the women on the team. Besides unique life experiences, they also understood better how a woman might think. Since many of the cold case victims were female, it made a big difference in how they proceeded.

The way he saw it, someone should start the meeting. So far, he was the only one except for Gus who had spent any time on it. Marcy presided over their former meetings due to being the actual detective in charge. No one questioned her authority because she happened to be a cop and had the needed experience. It wouldn't be all that easy for Jake. The last couple of cases took off without much input from him. Could be the other sleuths thought he wasn't all that interested.

He wiggled his shoulders, trying to shake off his unease. It reminded him of being picked last for the team in primary school. As a scrawny, awkward boy, athletic ability bypassed him in his early years. Later, his height and talent in pretending he knew something when he didn't, help create a new persona for him. Not being around folks that he grew up with was also an asset. Staying back and listening served. Tonight, he'd have to change his tactics.

Jake cleared his throat, trying to be heard over the competing conversations when a knock sounded. *Great Scott!* What now?

Chair legs scratched across the linoleum floor as Herman pushed back to answer the door. He cracked it only a little and his form blocked the view of whomever knocked. A low undecipherable murmur came from the hallway.

"Um…" Herman started. "Everything's okay. Thought we'd play a little gin rummy."

To hear better, every sleuth remained speechless, hoping to catch the other side of the conversation. Eunice even slipped out of her chair and crept closer to the door.

"I know it's late," Herman explained with his voice tightening with irritation. "This is my home, and I should be able to invite friends over if I please."

That time Jake could pick out a few words about *neighbors* and *being considerate*.

"We'll keep it down. No hooting with joy or victory dances," Herman offered and then said, "Goodnight!" as he closed the door.

Lola shot her husband a smile. "Good job, Hermy. As far as neighbors go, the unit to our right is empty. The Connors on our left take prescription sleeping pills about seven and sleep all through the night according to Mary, the wife. I doubt an earthquake could wake them. As for Mr. Caraballo, he listens to television so loud that I can pretty much quote all the dialogue from Matlock and Ironsides, which are two of his favorites."

Eunice returned to the table with a spark in her eye and a lifted chin. She shook one finger. "Imagine the staff warning *us* to be quiet. They get going some nights hooting and hollering like a pack of jackals announcing the kill. Here *she* comes and wants to know what *we're* doing."

This could easily morph from brainstorming to a complaint session. Fisting his hand, he rapped the wooden tabletop. "I think we need to remember the important thing is justice for Lyre. That's why we're here."

Surprisingly, everyone quietened at his knock. A survey of the table netted him a few nods of agreement. So far, so good. "We're here because it might help to share our thoughts about the case. What we know and what we don't know and anything that smells a little off."

"Ahem!" Eunice gathered attention. "Who put you in charge?"

This, he expected. When in doubt, go with the truth because lies would be too hard to keep straight. "I did. Without Marcy, we need some type of headship. At this point, I'm the person who has spent the most time with the case because I haven't been involved with the croquet tournament or squiring Hannah around the center."

"What?" Eunice's voice raised a bit, while Herman put out a flat palm and moved it in a downward motion as a reference to be quiet. In a softer, but no less perturbed voice, she asked, "What about the photos you took for the newspaper you're heading up now?"

That fabrication certainly hadn't served him well. Bitterness at Jake being picked to work on a newspaper while the activity director had rejected Eunice's suggestion of doing the same earlier remained. Truthfully, the director possibly feared a gossip rag or too much work on her part. "I told you before, that's my niece Katie's project. I'm only helping a little."

It would help if he reached Katie first and told her about her participation. As her only uncle, she indulged him. With any luck, the paper would fold after two issues.

Gus slapped the table, interrupting whatever barbs Eunice might have in store. "We're here to talk about the cold case. Let's do it. Strange goings-on, if you ask me."

It helped to have his friend back him up. Jake gave Gus a nod, then flipped open his notebook. By each bullet point, block letters listed all the inconsistencies with the case. He held up his ink pen, using it a bit like a pointer, stabbing the air as he spoke. "Lots of stuff missing from this case, which is to be expected with an unsolved case. Still, we have even more issues than most with this one. Did anyone notice anything unusual?"

Lola raised one finger from her place at the end of the table. "I don't want to sound like a ghoul," she wrinkled her nose at the word but continued, "Usually we have all these photos of the crime scene and the body. But instead, this time it's limited photos of the victim's home and a headless corpse."

Papers rustled as various sleuths checked out what Lola just said. Herman harrumphed after quickly pawing through the sheaf of information. "There's no medical report included."

"Yeah," Eunice added with enough vigor, rising halfway up in her seat. "Not only that, the body was never identified. This gobbledygook about how it *could* be her body is no kind of police work. Yeah, I read about the body being in the water. They could have done that mitochondrial DNA testing Hannah mentioned. It looks to me like we got nothing. Even her sister couldn't identify her, which seems weird. Surely her sister would know about childhood scars and more recent ones, too."

The woman had a point. Even though it coincided with a similar thought he had, it burned that Eunice managed to make the point before he did. Whatever he said would make him look like some Johnny-come-lately. Instead, he settled for tapping the pen on his notebook. "Good point. I looked up the mitochondrial DNA testing that you mentioned earlier. It appears to be a thing now. Apparently, even those family tree companies do it now for a price."

"Ah," Eunice pressed her hands together and grinned. "Somebody has been doing his homework. Hannah would be so proud."

The woman who was masquerading as someone else would be proud of him? Jake glanced down at his papers and snorted at the possibility. A prickling feeling like a fly walking across his skin brought his head up only to meet the disapproving stares of his friends. "What?"

Lola, who had made her way to the table and taken the chair by her husband, cleared her throat. "I don't understand why you're so hard on the woman. She's nice enough."

Really? Surely his friends, who prided themselves on their deductive skills, hadn't swallowed her act hook, line, and sinker? "Come on you guys. She's leading you on. What I don't understand is, what's her con? Do you seriously believe she's a washed-out astronaut's widow?"

"About as much as I believe you're a fighter pilot," Lola parried his question with an arch of her brows.

That stung. Both Herman and Gus knew he flew planes, but not necessarily what type. Maybe he should have corrected the first person who assumed he flew fighter missions as opposed to ferrying much-needed supplies, but after a while, he had bought into it, too. In a way, he was a bit like that cartoon dog imagining himself on dangerous missions. Part of him wanted to squeeze up into a tight ball and disappear under the door or any other convenient exit. Not knowing what to say, he growled, "What's your point?"

A chuckle escaped Lola as she directed an amused glance his way. "Don't get your blood pressure up. Consider that all of us are at a stage in our lives when all our big dreams are gone. In some ways we're like kids, imagining that we could be firemen, explorers, or ballerinas. The difference is we know it's not going to happen because most of our lives have already happened. What we do now is grasp for things that sound interesting, that give us some panache, or a little glamor." She pressed her manicured fingers against her chest as she continued.

"Look at me. I spent a few years as a showgirl in Vegas and that's how I'm remembered, not for the decades I spent in the unexciting world of real estate. Before you get stuck on the astronaut wife thing, take time to talk to Hannah. I imagine there's a reason behind her story. For all you know, she could have dated an astronaut before he went into space. Maybe she regretted not being part of that elite world. As for a con..." Lola shook her head slowly, "I know con artists and I can tell you she isn't one. Not so sure why you're so against her. I'd say you're acting like the stereotypical grumpy old man, always afraid someone's out to rip you off. You're better than that."

Grumpy old man. Stereotype. Certain everyone *was* out to scam him. Jake inhaled hard in an effort not to react. He prided himself on not being ordinary, but maybe he wasn't as extraordinary as he pretended. Just maybe Hannah found herself in a similar predicament. The sleuths remained silent, waiting for his response. Let them wait. Jake crossed his arms and tapped one foot before the iconic lightbulb glowed over his head.

"You're right. I *am* acting like a grumpy old man." Jake stuck his tongue out briefly and laughed. "My younger self would be so appalled. I swore I'd never become old, let alone a caricature of the old guy who yells at kids to stay off his grass. If Hannah comes back, I'll try to be less of a jerk." He held up his index finger. "I won't promise to not check out the Houston story."

The sleuths laughed, and then went back to listing oddities about the case. Gus cocked his head rather bird-like as he mused. "It's odd Lorelei didn't mention anything about identifying her sister when we dropped by tonight."

There were a few surprised glances, but nothing compared to Eunice's ramrod posture as she hissed, "You told me you went to buy me a present!" She sniffed and turned away from Gus, grumbling as she did so. "Soap. What kind of gift is that?"

The details of their fact-finding mission were bound to surface, but preferably not like this. Maybe Eunice didn't understand the specialness of the soap. "It's French-milled." He interjected, although he had no clue what it meant. "And it's…"

Lola unexpectedly held her hand up. "Stop now, Jake!" Her nose scrunched as she grimaced at the thought. "No woman wants soap as a gift. Keep that in mind the next time you decide to pick a token to show your love. Thank goodness Gus had enough sense to pick up chocolate. What I do want to know is what did you find out on your impromptu mission?"

A long breath escaped his pursed lips as he surveyed the avid stares of his fellow sleuths. Each one displayed some degree of curiosity, including Gus, who was there. However, it could be his friend wanted to see how he'd wiggle out of the situation.

His hand slipped back to rub his neck as he searched for possible explanations but abandoned them just as quickly. Jake settled for a simple shrug. "The original plan included Lance." He pointed to himself and Gus. "We thought up the Parrot Birthday Club as a way of getting our foot in the door. Lance probably thought Lorelei wouldn't kick out two old guys."

Gus hooted at the remark and slapped the table. "Shows how much *he* knows."

"Yeah," Jake had to agree, but it still stung that his parrot birthday party went so awry. Plenty of folks had parties for their pets.

Photos of confused dogs with a burning candlestick in their food along with angry cats in birthday hats demonstrated people threw parties for their pets. As a busy, single mother, Lorelei probably wasn't the type. Since she referred to the bird as Shut Up, their pet/pet owner relationship leaned toward problematic as opposed to doting.

Well?" Eunice wagged her finger. "What did you find out when you weren't giving bad advice about presents?"

"Yeah, what?" Gus asked as if he hadn't been there.

Jake cleared his throat and glared at Gus. "You *were* there."

"Right, right." Gus smoothed a hand over his head. "I guess I got caught up in the moment."

More likely he wanted to be on the side that wasn't being grilled. Jake flipped open his notebook. "As you know, there weren't too many notes from the case to go on. I heard some mention of Lorelei not being particularly close to Lyre. I doubt we were in the house for ten minutes and I received the impression the sisters had to be somewhat close."

"Why?" Herman was the first to ask the obvious.

"The parrot," Jake assured with a slight nod. "She knew her sister had the parrot and cared about it. Even though she's not fond of the animal, she's kept it all this time. We do know she asked for the parrot when the police investigated Lyre's trailer. Having met the parrot and listening to it chatter on about almost everything, I could understand Lorelei's irritation, but she didn't get rid of the parrot. It would be easy to sell such a valuable bird. The fact she held on to it could be sentimental because it's the last thing she had that belonged to her sister."

Most of the other sleuths either bobbed their heads or murmured their agreement, except for Gus. He pulled on one ear lobe before speaking. "It's not her bird. She has no right to get rid of it."

"Lyre is dead." Wasn't that the crux of the matter? Would there even be a crime if Lyre had just taken off? However, in his opinion, no one had put much effort into the case. It got swept out of the squad room like so many dead leaves.

"What if she isn't?" Gus asked with arched eyebrows and an eager expression.

When it came to kooky scenarios, Gus cooked up more than a few. Still, sometimes he was right. As much as Jake hated to go along with the idea, it did bear some consideration. Instead of addressing it head-on, he decided to lob the possibility to the group. "Okay, Sleuths, any opinions?"

Herman shook his head so hard that his wave of silver hair that he'd carefully combed back flopped across his forehead, while his wife settled for tapping her nails on the table.

A slight sniff came from Eunice. "I'm not partial to the idea of Lyre being alive. Maybe she faked her death. Could be she knew she was in trouble. The only way to get out was to vanish, which she did."

Good grief, the woman made sense. Worse, Jake found himself internally agreeing with her. "Would it be right to try to find someone who's running for her life?"

"Not find *her*," Lola tapped her finger against the Formica topped table. "We need to figure out who wants to kill her. I suspect once we figure that out, everything else will fall into place."

Lola had a point, as did Eunice and Gus. However, all those

points didn't add up to much. Jake cradled his weary head in his right hand and asked, "Anyone have a clue how we'll find who's gunning for Lyre?"

A few murmurs of frustration sounded while Lola pushed upright and worked her way into the kitchen, returning with the coffee pot. She reheated cups while holding onto the back of the chairs with her left hand to maintain her balance.

When she reached Jake, she teased, "It would be nice if the parrot could have told us."

That *would* be nice. Unfortunately, whoever the culprit was didn't hang around long enough to teach the bird.

Chapter Eighteen

A GENTLE LIGHT filled Jake's room, signaling it was morning. A gurgle, followed by a click, and then water dripping signaled his automatic coffee maker had switched on. The sharp squeak of the dietary cart passing in the hall confirmed the time. For some odd reason, those who weren't ambulatory ate before those who could walk to the dining room. He blinked a few times, trying to bring everything into focus. Hard to believe he once rolled out of his bunk at a whispered word from a fellow pilot and sprinted for his plane. Things were different then—not to mention being younger by a good fifty years or more. Now the morning consisted of getting his entire body on board with moving. His ears were working fine, although his eyes took a little longer.

Going to bed in the wee hours didn't help. Lola claimed the coffee was regular, but he'd swear otherwise. Keeping his eyes open during the meeting proved a trial, even with most of the Senior Sleuths being steamed because he and Gus chose to go out on their own to visit Lorelei. Hey, *they* were busy wooing Hannah. Someone had to handle the cold case.

He blew out a long breath before pushing upright and swinging his feet over the side of the bed. His bare toes touched the cold floor, causing him to jerk his feet back into the warm bed. Socks would eliminate the shock of the frigid floor. Still, where would it stop?

He'd soon be wearing a bed cap, too. His attention turned back to the Sleuths as opposed to his nightwear. They were upset with him but not as much as he expected.

Maybe he did decide to wing it on his own. Because he had a feeling that things might blow up in his face, he brought his buddy along. Gus epitomized the cute, old man with his wizened face, bald pate, and outrageous questions. Most folks humored him, never getting upset no matter what he said, except for Lorelei.

Before he left Herman and Lola's apartment last night, someone mentioned today's schedule. His brow furrowed as he tried to remember. Nothing. He couldn't think of a thing he needed to do. His whole day was wide open, which meant he could ponder the case and mention the newspaper to Katie. Since it wasn't official, maybe he'd only have to make a half-dozen copies to pass out. Still, something lingered at the back of his mind, rather like a stray cat, just out of reach.

The dietary staff would be passing out breakfast in the dining room soon. He needed to get a move on it. Grimacing before his toes touched the offending floor again, he forced himself to get out of bed. Jake shuffled toward the kitchenette at the same time as a lively knock sounded at his door.

"Wakey, wakey, Jakey!" a merry voice called out.

Gus. It should be against the law to be so happy this early. Jake reached for a cup to pour himself some wakeup juice. The knock sounded again. "I'm awake! I'll see you at breakfast."

"Not good enough. I need to see you now."

What was so important that it couldn't wait until they all met in the dining room? Had something happened in the night? Jake put down his cup and took four giant steps before lunging for the door and throwing it open. "Is Herman okay?"

"As far as I know," Gus said and strolled into the room, making his way to the wardrobe.

"Lola?" Jake asked, worried about the condition of each Senior Sleuth, which would be the only thing he'd accept as an excuse for the early morning visit.

Hangers complained as Gus pushed various items of clothing to the side after eyeing them. Gus interrupted his inspection to glance back at Jake. "I'd say she's doing much better. Hardly using her walker much. That's love for you. It can cure anything."

He pulled out a blue plaid shirt, glanced at Jake, and put it back.

While Gus could be a trifle unpredictable, his behavior leaned more toward peculiar this morning—more than usual. The only other person who could have taken a turn in the night was Eunice. If that were the case, Gus would be devastated. However, some folks handled grief in strange ways with denial being a principle coping mechanism. "Ah," Jake gentled his voice, "You feeling all right, friend?"

"Yep." He bobbed his head, then winked at Jake. "I'm a lucky man. Eunice was mad about our visiting Lorelei without her, but once I convinced her you were the one at fault, she forgave me. You could say we kissed and made up."

Knowing his friend could give way too many details, Jake held his hand up with the palm out to stop any further discussion on the matter. "Good for you. Still, don't get why you're in my room so early pawing through my clothes."

"Oh that!" He pulled out a black dress shirt and shot Jake an amused look. "Is this for the disco or those times you're pretending to be Goth?"

Jake grabbed the shirt and jammed it back into the wardrobe and slammed the doors shut. "Shopping time is over. I have no clue what you were looking for. All of my shirts would be too long for you."

"You're right." Not the least perturbed, Gus did a slow pivot, surveying the room. "Where's your old pilot bomber jacket with the wings, your rank, and name sewed on it?"

"That jacket is ancient. The only reason I keep it is for sentimental reasons. Wrapped it up nice and put it in the cedar chest."

"Okey dokey," Gus said as he headed for the long chest at the end of the bed. Before he could open it, Jake sat on it and folded his arms.

"It's too early for this nonsense so be quick and tell me what you're up to. I'd ask if you forgot to take your meds, but as far as I know, you're not on any."

"You're right about the meds." Gus also took a seat on the chest and stretched out his arms, interlacing his fingers. "The ladies thought I might help you pick out something appropriate to wear today."

Why didn't any of this make sense? Jake's lips turned down into a frown. "Why would the ladies care what I wear?"

Normally, Jake prided himself on his appearance. Unlike some of the residents, he knew not to mix patterns. After he saw a senior celebrity on television declaring that buttoned cuffs made a man look old, he started unbuttoning his cuffs and rolling them up the required four inches. Any more was too much, according to the fashion diva. Jake measured the area between his wrist and cuff to verify he had the exact length. Not only that, he applied the darkest night super black hair dye every month if he needed it or not.

Gus shifted on the chest, dropped his hands, and stared at them as if they were the most interesting thing he ever saw. "Well, ah, you better get dressed. I'm sure you'll pick something good to wear."

Jake would pick out something decent. He didn't have any worn, tattered shirts labeled as his favorite or lucky shirt. Some sports celebrities believed in that lucky shirt nonsense. The fools even bragged about their shirts being lucky, which upped the chance of them being stolen. No one knew about Jake's lucky boxers, and he planned on keeping it that way.

"Go on." He made a shooing motion in Gus's direction. "You not only need to grab your place but also let the staff know I'm coming so they can save a plate for me. You know the cooks gobble down anything left over. I saw one of the aides with a mounded plate of bacon one time. Your job is to go save my bacon."

Jake laughed, amused at his own pun. Gus didn't. Instead, he stood, walked to the door, gave Jake a backward glance, and murmured, "At least try. I'll tell them I tried."

The door closed softly, and Jake shifted into high gear, grabbing clothes, sipping coffee, and making a genuine effort to be on time. No reason to believe Gus would remind the staff to save him a plate. It should be a given since he ate in the dining room every day he'd been there, except for the time he stayed in his room to watch the royal wedding. That would stay his little secret.

Jake buttoned up the plaid shirt Gus had rejected. Apparently, a bee must have stung Gus where the sun doesn't shine. It had to have addled his thinking because there was nothing wrong with the blue plaid shirt. He carefully folded the cuff twice, which made it the correct length, as he considered the cold case.

As a top-notch investigative reporter, Lyre got the goods, but in doing so possibly angered folks. The type of folks she reported on were not the kind to turn the other cheek. It wasn't surprising that she ended up missing. The lack of public outcry he couldn't figure out, though. There wasn't even a press conference where the mayor swears he'll see justice done.

The only people still interested in Lyre were the tabloid reporters who bedeviled Lorelei. Jake peeked into his coffee cup and noticed he had a couple more swallows. It was sad that no one even cared about Lyre except for some scandal rag reporters. He lifted the cup to his lips, contemplating the reporters, when a revelation hit him so colossal that he jerked, spilling coffee on his shirt. "Sugar!"

He didn't have time for this. What he needed to do was share his sudden insight. He wet a rag and dabbed at his shirt, which transformed the tiny stain into a much larger wet circle. No time to change and it would dry before breakfast was over. Everyone would be so thrilled with his deductive skill.

Nurses with medicine carts, aides with food trays, and residents meandering along the hall constituted morning rush hour traffic. All it lacked was a custodian with a bucket headed his way. He spoke too soon because here came Wally, pushing the bucket via the mop that was immersed in the water. Not the best plan of action, but then Wally wasn't the best custodian. Jake's plan involved avoiding Wally and the doubtful bucket, but no one told the cheerful custodian.

"Mr. Jake! How are you this morning?" Wally moved closer, certain that most seniors couldn't hear. In doing so, he sloshed water onto Jake's pants leg and shoes.

A damp slash showed clearly on his khaki pants. Even though he'd been splashed with water of dubious origin, Jake managed a smile for Wally. "A bit damper than before, but I'll dry out. Gotta get to breakfast before they run out of food."

"You do that, Mr. Jake. I wouldn't want you to go hungry on my account." His face broke into a wide grin.

No one could stay mad at Wally. What he lacked in janitorial skills, he made up for with his genuine friendliness. Jake gave him a wave and turned into the dining room, but stopped at the sight of Hannah at his table. Gus's weird behavior suddenly made sense. If they thought to match him with Hannah, he had just put on the right outfit *not* to make a love connection.

As he neared the table, he heard Eunice relating their discussion of the night before, making sure to say several times she saw it on television last night.

Gus butted in with, "There were these tabloid reporters who kept wanting to talk to the dead girl's sister."

"Hmmm," Hannah nodded her head as if intrigued. "I bet those reporters weren't actually reporters."

How *dare* she steal his revelation without even realizing it wasn't a television show? The sleuths nodded at her conclusion, which resulted in Hannah laughing. Go ahead and laugh. First, she had taken his place at the table. His friends would be next. If that wasn't enough, she had just stolen his revelation. Too much Hannah for him, Jake turned to leave when Lola spotted him.

"Jake, what happened to you?"

So much for no one noticing a bit of water. He stepped forward, and his shoes squeaked. It was *more* than a bit of water. "It's a long story."

Hannah turned and arched one eyebrow and smiled, "I'd love to hear it."

Yeah, sure you would. That way you could use it in another one of your oh-so-amusing anecdotes. "I need to change."

Just when he was ready to exit with his dignity intact, a dietary aide carrying a breakfast tray beamed in his direction. "I've got your food. I even put extra bacon on it, as asked."

"Thanks." Sometimes, everything conspired against him. Looks like he was going to have to make nice with Hannah. On the plus side, she apparently had good insights, similar to his own.

Chapter Nineteen

THE CRISPY BACON crumbled as Jake bit into it. Even though he complained about Eunice, the woman got things done. Months ago, she'd roped Gus into a much-needed food protest. Jake had been supplementing his daily meals with peanut butter crackers and jerky sticks. Now, instead of snacks being the highlight of his day, it was the actual meals. Considering his former nemesis had good traits made him wonder about Hannah.

Chatter swirled about him about the upcoming croquet tournament. Surprisingly, many of the residents remained competitive in their senior years. As Eunice unrolled her strategy, he'd bet none of the seniors could hold a candle to her when it came to wiliness. Eunice eyed with each sleuth and Hannah as she spoke.

"I think we should all wear black and call our team the Undertakers or something equally morbid."

Lola shivered. "I don't know. There are unspoken rules here. You try not to mention death as much as possible since it's a constant but unwelcomed visitor at the center. Black isn't very flattering to me. It washes me out."

The newest addition to the table must have read the atmosphere wrong because Hannah offered her two cents. "They always wore white in Edwardian times when playing. The women had those big, oversized hats and the boys looked darling in their short pants and white shirts. Why not white?"

No one spoke for a moment, possibly waiting for the fallout from Eunice since the woman didn't like her ideas contradicted. A brief flash of anger flared in Eunice's eyes, which she quelled and then smiled with effort. "That was back when croquet was only for the rich. It didn't matter if they got grass stains on their clothes, since their servants laundered their clothes."

Since Jake hadn't delved into the history of croquet, he couldn't be certain if either woman was right. Every now and then, he liked to get Eunice riled. Oh, who was he kidding? He did it as much as possible. "Did the grass stains result from the knockdown fights that ensued over someone making a wrong call or taking an extra shot? I can just see them rolling around in the grass in their billowy white dresses, pulling hair."

Eunice narrowed her eyes and pressed her lips together, but Hannah laughed—a pure, unfettered sound of joy. The other sleuths giggled, which only caused the frown lines to deepen on Eunice's face. While Jake meant to tease, he hadn't meant to embarrass the woman, especially since she already had a bone to pick with him about suggesting soap as a gift.

"Oh, it wasn't that funny," he said, trying to stop the laughter.

Herman gave a final chuckle, while Gus slapped the table and got an elbow for his efforts. A napkin served as an impromptu handkerchief as Lola patted under her eyes. The last one to stop was Hannah, whose eyes danced with merriment. For a second, their gazes met. Jake could have sworn his heart stopped during that time. His hand pressed against his chest as he slowly inhaled. It couldn't be a heart attack. There was no family history of any. The fluttery sensation dropped from his heart to his stomach. Underneath his damp shirt, he could feel his heart beating away as usual. Not dying, that was good. What else could it be?

A possibility lurked in the back of his mind. No, not that! He refused to be sucked in like so many of the other marks. Besides eating breakfast, his job was to observe the devious con artist and not to fall for an easy laugh or even dark, mysterious eyes. That's how it started. A regular black widow spinning her web for the unwary with her fake stories.

Quickly over her minor upset, Eunice explained how they should undermine the other teams with their appearance and threatening name. Psychological tools helped, but practice won the game.

She clapped her hands together twice. "Okay, kiddies. We have all morning to work on our technique. I want to hear wood against wood."

More than one groan sounded. Even Hannah's cheery expression drooped a little. Maybe the woman didn't like croquet as much as she pretended. Hannah glanced down at her untouched breakfast. The downcast head revealed a vulnerable air. Part of her game, no doubt, but no one was watching her except him. With her head down, she didn't even respond to their rapid-fire conversation about the team names.

"I think it should be The Diablos," Herman suggested with a waggle of his eyebrows. "It will strike fear into our opposing teams."

Obviously, the idea didn't thrill Lola, who wrinkled her nose. "Oh no. That's typical male thinking. We should wow them with panache and style. Something glamourous would suit. "How about the Zeldas after Zelda Fitzgerald, who was known for her glamor and great parties?"

Gus harrumphed. "I'm not going to be any *Zelda*. Maybe we could go with an animal name like the sports teams. Instead of the wolves or bulldogs, how about something more appropriate like…" He paused, waiting to make sure he had everyone's attention before he said, "…the sloths."

Herman's mouth fell open, Lola grimaced, and Gus slapped the table. "Aha, good one! Sloths. because they're so…"

Before he could explain more, Eunice interrupted. "We know what sloths are."

In an unguarded moment, Hannah slipped her pinkie finger to her mouth and bit the nail. A nail biter? Jake blinked. It didn't fit with his image of a confidence woman. Kind of hard to imagine her selling overprice swampland as prime real estate while nibbling on her digits.

Pigeons, as the targets were often referred to, believed in the con because the scammer sold it so well with endless confidence and feigned friendship. It also appealed because it made the person feel important since the scammer commented on their honest face, intelligent eyes, or that they gave off the air of importance.

Jake pursed his lips as he considered the potential victims. If a person were smart, they'd smell a rat and would know better than to expect something from nothing. While this made sense, most folks harbored an underlying belief they'd win big someday, which explained gambling addicts.

Right now, Hannah's confidence and good humor vanished as the sleuths argued among themselves as they so often did. Being ignored didn't seem to bother the woman. If anything, he had the impression by the nail chewing that she might be a tad anxious.

Good manners dictated he say something since he wasn't involved in the name discussion.

"Did you drive yourself or did your children drop you off?"

The hand dropped from her mouth, her head turned in his directions, she blinked, and then blushed. Most folks might have missed it with her olive skin tone, but Jake registered the heightened color. Either the woman was shocked to find him sitting there or embarrassed to be caught chewing her fingernail. He assumed it was the latter.

"Ah, I drove. No children." She dropped her head again, which made Jake wonder if this was a sore spot. He tapped his chest.

"Same here. No children." Would a con artist say they didn't have kids or would children be more of a touchpoint with their victims? Nevertheless, he didn't offer his childless state until after she did. It could be she wasn't trying to con anyone and merely padded out her back history to sound more interesting, Still, acting anxious could be part of the game. So hard to tell, but as a sleuth, he needed to get to the bottom of it. One thing he had learned from working with both Lance and Marcy was that the unexpected questions often yielded results. What question would do that? Before he could concoct an unexpected inquiry, Hannah did.

"Is that why you decided to move to the center? Because of the loneliness?" she asked in a voice softer than her previous tone.

An unexpected question—he'd have to give her the point. Talk about personal. It said more about her than it did him, didn't it? Why *had* he moved here? "Gus asked me to move to the center. His plan was to get the three amigos back together. Herman, Gus, and I were all in the service together."

She nodded. "It must be nice to have that type of friendship—a bond that has lasted over decades."

His shoulders went up in a shrug. "Never thought of it that way, but you're right. We may not always agree, but I trust both. You can't say that about too many people."

Jake thought his comment had just the right amount of barb to it, implying he didn't trust her. Would she get the nuance? The woman sighed and gave a small nod. "Treasure that. I had a few friends like that. Miriam and Candace."

"What happened to them?" he asked before weighing his question. Was this another yarn she was spinning? Even so, she wouldn't be getting any money off him. Herman would testify to that fact since Jake seldom contributed gas money for their various jaunts.

"Life," Hannah answered, staring at the wood-paneled wall.

Perpetrators usually gave themselves away with elaborate explanations and alibis. Most people didn't make a point of calling several people or being seen in a public place that had security cameras to establish an alibi. Only the guilty worked that hard to establish their whereabouts. Going home after work and watching television alone might not be provable, but was most likely the truth. Maybe life *did* get in the way. While Jake had been friendly with several people, he just as easily fell out of touch due to job switches or relocations.

"Miriam died from pancreatic cancer. For her sake, it was quick or I should say quick once it was diagnosed. We'd been meeting for lunch every Wednesday for years. In the last couple of months, she complained about an upset stomach. We joked about our favorite restaurant losing its best cook. We never realized at the time it was a symptom."

Any fictional detective would have a granite jaw and be unwilling to be pulled into the sob story. Jake leaned in Hannah's direction to pat her lightly on the shoulder. "Sorry to hear that. What happened to Candace?"

If it was another sad story, he'd be on his guard.

"Oh." Her shoulders went up in a shrug. "I wonder that myself. Candance *did* have children. We used to talk about joining one of those women's groups that wear red or purple hats and go places like plays, dinners, and even trips together."

This story wasn't shaping up to be a cry fest. "Did Candace die?"

"Depends on how you look at it." Her lips tugged up in a wry expression, and she sniffed. "Candace had a daughter who moved out west and produced the standard two offspring. Even though Candace and I had planned to do all these things together, she took off to play grandma twenty-four-seven. I called there a few times just to make sure she was okay. You know when someone doesn't call you, you worry."

Jake murmured an acknowledgment and motioned for her to continue.

"Well, I'd call every few weeks to see how she was doing. On a rare occasion, she'd call me. It may have taken me a while to realize she had no interest in the life she'd left behind here in Indiana."

The earlier loneliness comment felt authentic. The stories rang true or they *could* be a lie she'd honed over the years, perfecting her acting skills. The best way to test it would be to ask more questions. Even the novice criminal has a cover story, but the deeper you dig, the more the tale starts to unravel.

Residents strolled or rolled out of the dining room, casting interested glances in their direction. News wise, not much happened at the center, with the biggest recent event being Herman and Lola's flying to Vegas to get hitched. Could be a few wondered about the unlikely married couple or were curious about Hannah's presence.

His fellow sleuths, instead of being concerned about the cold case, continued to bat names around. Herman suggested, "The Edwardian Players?"

His name garnered an eye roll and a snort from Eunice. "That makes us sound like a theater group or very strange playboys."

From outside appearances, Eunice ruled the roost, but she'd eventually compromise to a certain extent. First, there had to be the debate. Jake returned his attention to Hannah, thinking of a probing question. "What was Miriam's occupation?"

Since there was no mention of children, the woman couldn't be a stay-at-home mother. He expected astronaut wife, to which he'd follow up with, which astronaut? Then he'd check it out online.

"Librarian, elementary school librarian." Hannah gave a wistful smile. "She even told me all about it. The little ones were so excited about reading, not like the older high school students, who usually only came into the media center to do research. Most of the time they were either trying to visit game sites, listen to music, or look at porn. There were a few who actually did research."

Jake's eyebrows arched as she rattled off all the things the older students did. It was peculiar she talked so much about the older students since her friend dealt with just the younger ones. A lightbulb popped on over his head, but he had a few more questions to test his theory.

"What's a media center? I don't think they had one at my small school."

Hannah wrinkled her nose and chuckled. "I'm sure they did, only they called it a *library*. The difference now is computers make up most of the libraries, which are now called media centers. Often, LCD projectors are hanging from the ceiling for presentations. Librarians are referred to as media specialists. I prefer the title *librarian* since it has a bit of gravitas and history behind it."

Her voice had risen in volume as she expounded on the modern library, garnering the attention of the other sleuths who had turned her way. Now it was time for the final question. "Was Candace also a librarian?" He cleared his throat, knowing he had made a verbal misstep, "I mean, a media specialist?"

The color flared in Hannah's cheeks, and she glanced back at the other sleuths before meeting Jake's eyes. "Oh no, she was my assistant. If the school is big enough, you can have an assistant. I guess that's why I felt betrayed when she moved away after spending two decades working together."

Aha! She might as well have said she *was* a librarian. Wait, didn't she just do that? Jake glanced over at the rest of the sleuths for signs of shock or disapproval. Nothing. If anything, Gus grinned, and Lola tried to hide her amusement behind her hand.

"You all knew?"

Hannah touched his arm. "I'm sorry. When Herman and Lola suggested I pretend to be someone I wasn't, I thought it would be fun. I did a little theater in college. I had no clue it would become so involved. Being a lifelong reader and writer, I do have a vivid imagination."

He huffed. "No wonder everyone acted so sure you weren't a confidence woman here to flim-flam us."

Earlier fears about Hannah vanished, but his ire at his friends remained. "Why?"

"We thought it would shake you out of the rut you've been in," Herman admitted. "You remind me of a basset hound with your long face. I can't remember the last time you laughed. You're a regular Debbie Downer."

Debbie Downer. He couldn't believe Herman called him that. Before his romance with Lola, Herman had to have been the dourest one in the group. Now he was pointing the finger at Jake. Love had transformed his friend into a much happier man. Still, it didn't seem fair for the newlywed to poke fun at the unattached guy's expense. His brow furrowed, and his lips turned down as he considered Herman's casual remark.

Had he been in a rut? More like a pity party. "Okay. You've had your fun. Remember, your time is coming, but I'm glad to clear my plate of the fake astronaut wife bit. We have more important things to do."

"You're so right," Eunice agreed and stood. "Dominoes! Assemble!" She clapped her hands together.

"Dominoes?" Jake repeated the word, uncertain how it fit into the conversation and unsure if he wanted to know.

Lola pointed a lacquered nail in his direction. "Dominoes is our croquet team name. You'll need a black and white spotted top. If you don't have one, bleach dispensed with an eyedropper can create one from a black shirt. If you create your own, you can choose your own number by how many dots you make. Got a clue how many dots you want?"

The last thing he wanted to do was to drop eye droppers of

bleach onto a perfectly good shirt. "Zero. I want zero dots."

"Sounds about right," Eunice said and then chortled.

Jake refused to speak any further. It would just give the group another opportunity to pull a joke on him. In his opinion, everyone had overused their options to tease, trick, or ridicule him in some fashion. The only problem was if he pointed this out, he *would* be a Debby Downer.

Chapter Twenty

JAKE LEANED AGAINST the sun-warmed brick building, clutching his wooden croquet mallet. Normally, he'd rather be doing anything else than chasing a wooden ball through patchy grass of the Greener Pastures' courtyard. Right now, he'd make an exception. Apparently, Eunice's no-boundaries mouth got her in trouble when Lola took offense. The former showgirl could go toe to toe with anyone and usually did when she felt like it. Only now, Herman felt he should be part of the defense team.

The women were almost touching noses as they hurled insults at each other. An anxious Herman kept shuffling around the combatants, wringing his hands. "Are they usually like this?" Hannah inquired as she joined Jake in holding up the building.

Good question and not the easiest to answer. "No." Well, that was partly untrue. If Hannah did elect to move in, she'd discover the truth. "Sometimes, they're worse." His shoulders went up in a shrug. "Nothing ever comes of it."

"Too much drama for me." An audible exhale escaped Hannah. "I came over here to apologize. I'll admit the astronaut's wife thing was my idea. I took it from a book I'm writing."

"You write?" Jake's eyebrows lifted. "Is this the truth or did they send you over to play another joke on me?"

"Ah, I probably deserve that." Her gaze dropped to the ground, and she kicked at a loose clod of dirt. "Trust me. My writing isn't all that exciting. I decided after watching about the five hundredth crime drama, I could write better tales. All the latest forensic techniques are embedded in my brain. Besides, I've read thousands of books as a librarian—not all mysteries, though."

"Would I have read anything you wrote?" Jake enjoyed a good read before retiring for the night. Personally, the librarian turned author was much more appealing than Con Woman. A chuckle greeted his question. Hannah wrinkled her nose and turned toward him.

"The only way that could have happened is if you had broken into my house, booted up my computer, and read my stories. Somehow, I can't see you doing that."

"Yes," he agreed. "It would be hard since I don't know where you live."

Her index finger touched her lips as if she were about to urge herself to silence, then she dropped it. "You might know my address in a couple of days or so. I'm considering moving in."

Even though more than a hundred people chose to call the center home, it surprised Jake that Hannah would be one of them. She didn't seem the type, but then again most of the sleuths failed to fill the stereotypical senior citizen profile. He couldn't think of one of them who enjoyed puzzles, and no one crocheted to his knowledge. He cut his chin in the direction of the argument.

"I'm sure Eunice's competitiveness cinched the deal, or was it Gus's love of a practical joke?"

"Neither." She shook her head and pressed her fingers against the brick wall. "I think it was you."

"Ha." A laugh popped out at the ridiculousness of her reply.

"I've been surly, and according to Herman, either resembled or acted like a basset hound. How'd that convince you?"

"Oh, you haven't been all *that* bad." A smile danced across her face and vanished as quickly as it came. "I'm glad you were suspicious of me and protective of your friends. It says a great deal about you. When I was doing my little act about being the astronaut's wife, I tried to be peppy and on all the time. Always the big smile no matter what."

While it would be a lie to say he didn't enjoy her smile, too much cheery good humor tended to put his back up some. No one acted that way twenty-four-seven unless they were finagling to get something or possibly wanted to make a good impression.

Herman had turned to face the door, as did the other three. Whoever was there had their attention. A small dog dashed across the grass and headed toward Lola, who managed to scoop up the canine with Herman's help. Moving slower and much more elegantly was the black and white cat Eunice had snuck into the center.

"I didn't know you could have pets here," Hannah remarked with an upraised eyebrow. "I don't have one myself, but I might be interested in getting one if it's a possibility."

Even though Jake pretended not to care about the animals, he still squatted and whistled, hoping to lure one of the pets his way. Not attracting nearly as much attention, Lance and Marcy strolled toward the group with their arms linked. If they hoped for an update on the cold case, they'd be disappointed. Not only did they have precious little to share, but they also had to keep quiet in front of Hannah. He cleared his throat, remembering he'd failed to reply.

"Pets are a tricky issue. The director somewhat likes the idea of animals interacting with the residents. We have pet visits at least once a week." He tried to remember the details of their center pet or pets. "We had a center pet once. A rabbit. I heard it hopped right on out of the building one day. I think they had hoped to make the cat Domino there into a center pet."

As soon as he said the cat's name, Jake realized their team had been named after Eunice's beloved stray cat.

"What happened?" Hannah prompted, unaware Jake's mind had taken a left turn from the subject.

"Well, I, um, what were we talking about?" His face flushed. He hated it when he forgot things. Then he remembered—the cat. "We were talking about the cat. I think most residents remember having a pet. Turns out if the residents can be competitive about a game of croquet, they can be competitive about pets, too. Some of the residents would nab Domino and keep him enclosed in their room as a personal pet."

"I can see that might be an issue."

"Yeah. Soon, people were demanding their own pets, but that put the kibosh on Domino. Board of Health wouldn't care for us having our own Wild Kingdom here. There'd be pet fights. Dogs chasing cats. Litterboxes that needed cleaning along with general pet care. That's why we have pet *visits*. Only an animal that couldn't escape might work, which might explain the hundred-gallon aquarium on H wing."

Laughter and conversation floated on the air as the sleuths chit-chatted with Marcy and Lance. A few tidbits reached Jake, and in turn, Hannah.

"Not much on the cold case. We had a confab the night before."

"Still, not buying no one could identify the body."

Jake coughed, then pushed off the wall and stood in front of Hannah as if that would somehow distract the woman. An elderly man in mussed clothes seldom ranked when a more provocative topic existed nearby. "So, what are you going to do to prepare to move?"

"My house is already sold." She leaned slightly to the left to peer around Jake.

That wouldn't do. He did a neat sidestep and grinned, not knowing how to explain his actions. "What about your belongings? You can bring furniture. Some folks believe it makes their unit cozier. What about your car?"

He assumed she had a car since she mentioned driving. All he had to do was keep talking to distract her. What if he ran out of things to say? It could happen. Jake shoved his hands into his pants pockets and started jingling his change. Mentally, he was reviewing what he'd say next as opposed to listening, which was a definite no-no. He did catch one word. *Lighthouse.* "What did you just say?"

Hannah sniffed, held out her right hand and inspected her cuticles. "You weren't paying attention."

"I was trying to come up with more questions to keep the conversation going." He gave the change in his pockets a hard jingle.

"No one wants questions thrown at them like they're being given the third degree." She pointed up to the sky. "All that's missing is a bare bulb over my head."

Maybe she had a point. Most of his conversation with women consisted of empty flattery and usually agreeing with whatever they said without paying a great deal of attention. Eunice was his exception since he neither flattered her or agreed with her if he could help it. "Ah, you're right. I'm sorry, but I did hear the word lighthouse. What were you saying about a lighthouse?"

In landbound Indiana, there were no lighthouses. Peculiar that Hannah should mention a lighthouse when the parrot kept repeating *lighthouse* and four numbers.

"I'm surprised that word caught your ear. Makes you sound more like a sailor than a pilot." She arched one eyebrow and smirked. Instead of elaborating, she kept silent.

Heavens to Betsy, he knew good and well the woman said nothing as payback for not listening. "I did apologize, which should count for something."

"Hmm, you say something?"

"You know I did. Would you please tell me about the lighthouse?" Thank goodness no one else could witness his begging.

"Sure." Hannah crossed her arms and nodded her head. "Since you asked so nicely, I'd be glad to. Anyhow, I was saying even though I was moving out of my house, there's so much I'm not ready to let go. I don't have any children to hand stuff off to, so why not store it? Eventually, I'll probably toss it or sell it, but for now, I rent a unit at Lighthouse Rental. You may have seen it by the overpass. It has a lighthouse at the top with a rotating light. It's a pretty new place, not run down like some of those other places."

A mental alarm sounded in Jake's head. A storage facility would be the perfect place to hide information, but Hannah mentioned it was new. "How long has it been around?"

One hand slipped up to massage her neck as her eyes rolled up.

"Probably three or four years."

"That's it!" It fit the time frame. Now all he had to do was check it out and discover who rented 4106. "You're a genius. I could kiss you." After running details through his head and getting nothing, this was the breakthrough he needed.

"It was nothing." Hannah blinked. "Not sure what's so great about a storage facility."

Jake impulsively bent forward and kissed Hannah's cheek. "*You're* what's great."

Her hand covered her cheek, and she shot him a saucy look. "I've been warned about you. Eunice calls you a love 'em and leave 'em type."

"I've been called worse." Jake shrugged his shoulders, delighting in the repartee, but at the same time wanting to relay the information about the storage facility and find out if the police could open it up. It may need to be opened by other means. If only Lance and Marcy would join them, he could introduce Hannah, then give them a hand signal he had important information. Too bad they never developed a gesture for *that*.

Chapter Twenty-One

THE SUN CLIMBED a little higher, flooding the people below with bright autumn light and a modicum of heat. Laughter and conversations filled the small, open-air courtyard contained within the Greener Pastures Convalescent and Retirement Center. A small dog frolicked across the grass, pulling smiles from nearby watchers. An artist specializing in feel good portraits might entitle the scene *Leisurely Afternoon*. Jake would call it *Awkward Moment*. Maybe it would be better to call it *Never-Ending Awkward Moment*. Usually in a situation like this, you could walk away and never again see the person in question. Not a possibility. He wasn't even certain he wanted it to be a possibility. After all, Hannah, eager to make friends at the center, played along with the shenanigans after possibly being assured it was all in good fun.

Lance ambled over to where Jake and Hannah stood uncomfortably beside one another in front of the building wall. On arrival, Lance nudged Jake and said, "Aren't you going to introduce me to your new friend?"

From his tone, he might as well have added *wink, wink*. Anyone overhearing the conversation might mistakenly assume Jake and Hannah were an item. Nothing could be farther from the truth. Currently, they were civil now that he'd concluded he had nothing to fear from the woman as far as cons go. Her sharp mind and wit could make things interesting. Unlike some of the female residents who could be won over by a hackneyed line, Hannah would see right through it.

"Lance." He turned in the detective's direction as he spoke, and then gestured to the enigma next to him. "This is Greener Pastures' soon-to-be newest resident, Hannah…" He paused, not remembering her name.

"Holt." Hannah offered with a smile and an outstretched hand. "Like the female private eye from the 1980s detective show."

Jake watched while the two shook hands and engaged in casual chit chat. Holt might be the name of a detective, but he doubted Hannah had any claim on it. He might not remember the first name she used, but he knew it wasn't Holt. What was the likelihood of her name being the same as a television detective?

In the distance, he could see both Marcy and Lola seated on a bench interacting with Bear, the ironically named toy dog Herman snuck into the center to impress Lola. Close to the bench stood Gus and Eunice, the latter cradling Domino, the cat, like a baby. Hannah's delicate laughter caused Jake to be drawn into the conversation. It wouldn't be eavesdropping since he was only a foot or so away.

"Oh, you're a detective. How nice!" Hannah basically cooed the words. "I consider myself an amateur sleuth, but I do all my crime-solving on a laptop."

"I've heard," Lance countered, making Jake wonder how the detective knew so much. Could be he avoided the astronaut's wife nonsense and mined actual information as opposed to being the brunt of a joke.

Lance released Hannah's hand and maintained eye contact while tapping his index finger against his temple. "Where do most of your ideas come from?"

"Almost everywhere." Hannah pressed her hands together as she spoke. "Sometimes, I see a movie that I think could have been better, and I rewrite it. Other times it's a news story, and every now and then, it's an overheard conversation that sparks a plotline. Her eyes twinkled as she explained. "If all else fails, I play a game of what if or what would make it worse?"

The last part of that made Lance chuckle. "Yes, I've heard writers tend to torture their characters."

Just his luck that the two got along as well as peanut butter and jelly. It would be difficult to get Lance's attention outside of jumping in front of Hannah and waving his arms as if directing a 747. Blocking the woman would be weird and rude, but maybe if he just got closer, the detective, being an observant individual, would notice the action and naturally assume Jake had important news. He took a side step closer, trying to catch Lance's eyes. His movement went unnoticed by the detective. However, Herman, who had sauntered to their side of the courtyard, snorted.

"Geesh, Jake. Give the woman some space. We can't have you running her off. We need her in the Senior Sleuths."

No, he couldn't have. Jake's hand drifted to his jaw to ascertain if his mouth hung open at the statement. It did. He snapped it closed with an audible click of his molars. They didn't know the woman from Eve. Were they just going to let her be part of the group? After all, he had to...he searched his mind for what arduous tasks he undertook to be a part of the group. The best he could remember was Marcy invited him. Yep, that was pretty much it.

"Herman." He moved away from Hannah as he spoke and closer to his friend. When he was almost six inches away, he lowered his voice. "It's not your place to decide who's in the group. It's Marcy's place."

"Who do you think sent me over here?" Herman waggled his shaggy brows, then slapped Jake on the shoulder. "Lighten up, pal. Don't take everything so seriously. With Marcy gone, we could benefit from someone who has a handle on forensic science, which it sounds like Hannah does. The way our current case is bumping along, or should I say *not* bumping, we need Hannah's help."

Before Jake could reply, Hannah did. She cupped her hands over her ears and said, "My ears are burning. Someone must be talking about me."

"Um..." Herman started, a little flustered at being caught. "A little. It was all good. I was telling Jake how we need your crime-solving skills."

How could everyone be missing the obvious? Unfortunately, it would be up to him to spell it out, which would make him into a curmudgeon, a role he didn't covet for himself. Jake smoothed down his shirt, tugging on it a little as he spoke. "Her *fictional* crime-solving skills. She writes about a crime, then has her main character solve it. That doesn't make her a member of the police department. I bet her sleuth solves the crime every time."

"Okay," Hannah replied in a sharp tone. Her fingers rubbed her forehead as if a headache might be coming on. "I don't claim to be a best-selling author, but I do my research. If you bothered to listen, I explained to Lance how many different sources I use. As for my main character solving the crime every time, that's sort of the premise of the mystery genre. Jessie, my main character, is haunted by the murder she couldn't solve—the car bombing that killed her brother."

Maybe her characters were more complex than he had originally thought. A tingling feeling like bugs crawling over his skin occurred due to the combined censorious stares of both Herman and Lance. It didn't take a mind reader to know they were annoyed with him. Still, why should they just roll over and invite Hannah into the group? What if she was a spy pretending to move into the center to infiltrate the group to find out what they knew?

Jake crossed his arms. Just wait until Hannah informed her boss and things went south in a hurry. In his mind, he pictured Herman begging his forgiveness for his failure to listen. Of course, there was one thing wrong with his scenario. It depended on Hannah *knowing* about the case. Outside of the sleuths, only Marcy and Lance knew. Never mind the minor detail of Hannah being in cahoots with whoever took Lyre.

What worried him more was this would be the *All Hannah Show* with all her knowledge about forensic sciences and cutting-edge technology. This was supposed to be Jakes's chance to shine. The last thing he needed was for Hannah to take over the case. While he might not be a fan of sharing credit, Eunice hated it more and was fond of mumbling something about keeping your friends close and your enemies closer. Jake wasn't sure which one she considered him, possibly the latter. Still, as a strategy, it had merit.

He could stomp his feet like a disappointed five-year-old when a game didn't go his way, and then head off to his room, which would result in his not being on the case. What he needed to accomplish was sharing his clue that important evidence could be hidden at Lighthouse Rental. Then, everyone would be appropriately appreciative if his clue proved true. First, he had to get to the Lighthouse storage units. This required someone with a car and who knew where the place was located.

Herman used to be his go-to person when it came to driving, but once he got married everything became a *We* decision involving both Herman and Lola. Right now, the other half of the decision-making team fussed over Bear, the dog. No way would she be a fan of cutting the pet visit short.

The only other people who arrived in a vehicle were Marcy and Lance, who had brought the pets. When they were ready to leave, they'd take the pets home, which could mean there might not even be room in the car with the animal carriers.

A heavy sigh escaped Jake. He could call a cab, but it still left him without a reason for even being at the rental place. What he needed was a legitimate excuse, such as moving and needing to check out the place before renting a storage unit.

Actually, he knew someone who was moving and might have even been to Lighthouse Rental. His gaze drifted to Hannah, who was still chatting with Herman and Lance. How in the world could he convince her to take him to the storage unit? His index finger automatically smoothed his eyebrows as he thought. Living in the center brought him face to face with too many out of control eyebrows, and he refused to be numbered among the group.

His teeth worried his lip as he turned over possible scenarios. All he came up with was asking her. Talk about a crazy plan, but it was all he had. Now he would bide his time, which was no easy thing while admitting any other sleuth could come up with the same revelation.

Lola gestured for Herman, who hurried to his sweetheart's side. *One down*, Jake couldn't help thinking. Eventually, Lance bid Hannah goodbye with a promise to meet again. Time to act. Jake sidled closer rather like a spider.

Before he could say anything, Hannah did, "Spit it out! I could see you were waiting for the others to leave to have your say. Quite frankly, I don't have time to pussyfoot around the subject. You strike me as a man who appreciates straight talk."

"I do," Jake acknowledged. What he hadn't expected was Hannah to react the way she did. "I can use your help."

"Oh really?" Hannah arched a brow, crossed her arms, and leaned back against the building. "This I want to hear. Now, tell me what little ol' me can do for you?"

This must have been how the mouse in the folk tale felt when he stumbled across the lion with the hurt paw. As he remembered, the mouse survived, which might bode well for him. "Well, I was wondering if you would drive me to Lighthouse Rental to have a look around. It's about a cold case. Could be a clue."

"Allll rightttt…" she lengthened the words, but it could have been an acknowledgment he heard as opposed to an agreement to drive Jake anywhere. "Why not ask Herman?"

Right now, he wished he had. "Lola loves to visit with Bear. Herman snuck him into the center for her. It would be cruel to cut their time short."

"Seems fair," Hannah inclined her head, but her expression remained unconvinced. "What else?"

Smart women could be a trial, always seeing through flimsy excuses. "I want to check out my assumption before presenting it as fact. It will save everyone a great deal of time."

"It will help you save face, too." Hannah pushed off from the wall.

Jake found himself missing the cheery astronaut wife who smiled way too much, but at least this incarnation of Hannah bore an air of authenticity. "Yeah, that too."

"Since you're being honest with me, I'll do it. I feel like I owe it to you, allowing myself to be talked into that trick. If you're ready we can head out now."

"Ready!" Jake called out. The drive over could be a new start for the two of them, rather like those sitcoms when people started out on the wrong foot, went out the door, closed it behind them, then rang the doorbell to start again. He only hoped Hannah could forget his earlier behavior. On the other hand, she struck him as having a good memory.

Chapter Twenty-Two

JAKE AND HANNAH exited the courtyard with very little fuss. The Senior Sleuths waved them on. Even Eunice held up Domino's paw and moved it as if he were bidding them farewell instead of scolding them about missing practice. As a resident familiar with the rabbit warren of twisted hallways that tangled through the center, Jake guided Hannah with a word or a gesture until they reached the front door. Normally, if traveling with Eunice or Gus, his exit became much more cloak and dagger since the two weren't allowed to leave the center without previous permission.

With Hannah, he held the exterior door open for her, and the two of them left like regular folks with the receptionist not even glancing up from the cell phone in her hand. It must be the attitude. He filed away the observation for future further examination. Residents could go outside, sit on the porch, or walk the acres of landscaped ground. It's when the residents who were checked in by family put a toe beyond the property line that the excitement began. Well, not all the time, Jake mentally corrected his summation. Besides the Sleuths, there were a few adventurous spirits who strolled the nearby neighborhood and returned without anyone being the wiser.

The two of them strode with purpose as if they had an entire agenda to work through before they slept. Being busy made Jake happy. When he did work a nine to five job, he often complained about it, especially when he worked past quitting time. Often, he fantasized about retirement and how he'd be able to sleep late and do nothing all day.

Hannah surprised him by speaking. "What are you thinking about that has you looking so glum? I hope it isn't the thought of riding along with me."

"Retirement, back when I was working, I couldn't wait for retirement. My days were so full that I looked forward to long stretches of doing nothing."

"And now?" Hannah prompted as they stepped onto the black-topped surface.

"I've rested plenty. Now I'd prefer busy. Not crazy busy like I was when I was forty, but something more than taking afternoon naps and watching reruns of shows I used to like." He gave her a curious look, interested in how she might respond about being younger.

"I hear ya. Kept busy all my life. Education is a good career if you want plenty of filler work. Most people think you go to school at eight and return home at three." A laugh broke free. "I think many women went into teaching because they thought they'd have a long vacation to spend with their children."

"They don't?" Jake, too, had assumed as much.

"Nope." Hannah gave an emphatic shake of her head. "For whatever reason, there's always a great deal of movement, cleaning, and construction over breaks. I spent plenty of time prepping the media center. Then, I had to come in before school started and unpack everything. There's also continuing education hours, in-services, and more staff meetings for the upcoming school year.

She pointed her thumb back at herself, "As a media specialist, administration assumed I was sitting in the library twiddling my thumbs. Anything that went on at the school, I was somehow involved in from registration to the art fair."

"Art fair?" Jake echoed her words.

"Uh-huh," Hannah murmured as she picked her way around some oversized SUVs decorated with stick people figures or round medallions announcing how many miles they had run or where they'd vacationed. It reminded Jake of those saving stamps books where, when you got enough stamps, you could trade in for merchandise. What did the owners of the decorated cars get when they covered all their windows?

Light reflected off the windows and shiny exteriors of the various cars in the parking lot. Jake surveyed the sedans and the occasional pickup truck, speculating which vehicle Hannah drove. You could tell a lot about a person by what they drove. Hannah came to a stop beside a smaller box-like version of a SUV. Even though he'd seen a ton of these vehicles on the road, he wasn't too sure what to think.

A beep sounded before a slight click indicated his door had unlocked. Jake opened it and slid into the warm exterior while Hannah did the same on her side. Boxes crowded the back where the seats had been pulled down to create more hauling space.

Once both doors were closed, Hannah started the car and switched off the oldies rock station that had been playing. As she maneuvered out of the parking lot with ease, she returned to their interrupted conversation. "Too many evenings alone is the reason I'm considering Greener Pastures. At work, I saw people every day. Retired, I only see anyone when I go shopping. I became concerned when I realized I had a favorite cashier at the grocery. If she was working, I'd get in her line no matter how long it was because I wanted to talk to her. That's when I decided I need more social interaction."

A legitimate reason to enroll in a retirement center. Still, he thought women belonged to all these social groups. "Aren't there a lot of ladies groups out there?"

"Some," Hannah agreed as she pulled out onto the main road after a generous opening in the traffic presented itself. "Most of those groups are for young women to get a break from their kids. The others are rather cliquey. Many have been friends since grade school and aren't open to new members. I belong to a book group that meets online due to distance and aging members not being able to drive in the dark. While I enjoy our once a month book club online, I can't build a life around it. Marcy is the one who suggested Greener Pastures."

Talk about being left out of the loop. "How did you meet Marcy?"

A pickup truck whose chassis loomed about two feet above its oversized tires swerved around them, causing Hannah to murmur under her breath. "Morons."

"Yeah, I know," Jake concurred.

After turning onto a less busy road, Hannah spoke. "Hospital."

People thought *he* was cryptic. Jake turned in his seat, trying to locate a hospital. None. Most of the businesses were single-story dwellings consisting of restaurants, quickie marts, and the occasional tractor or pet supply place. There were no high-rise medical facilities around and as far as he could tell, no emergency medical places, either. "I don't see a hospital."

"You asked how Marcy and I met. We met in the hospital. At first, she was in ICU and they were downgrading her to a private room. Turns out there wasn't one, so we shared a room for a few days. I did most of the talking because she was despondent. At the time, I would have thought she didn't hear anything I said, but she obviously did, since she contacted me later. She did so about every couple of months or so. Gave me the credit that I kept her going, which I doubt. Anyhow, when I mentioned a retirement community, she suggested Greener Pastures."

That meant Hannah knew Marcy longer than he did. No wonder Marcy okayed Hannah's entrance into the group. It also meant Lance and Marcy had plenty of time to run her personal history. "How did you come up with the astronaut story? Or was that Herman's plan?"

A large faux lighthouse squatted on a single-story building surrounded by small garage units. The blinker sounded before Hannah turned into the business. "Oh, that was from one of my stories. My investigator pretends to be an astronaut's wife to investigate a crime at an aerospace firm. We're here." She cut the engine. "What do I need to know before I go in and ask to look at the units?"

Jake cut his eyes to the boxes behind him. "You could say you're moving in today. Maybe you'd want a unit as close to 4106 as possible. It could be your favorite number."

"Okay, I'll do it on one condition." Hannah gave him a skeptical look that promised more questions would follow.

He'd been around Eunice long enough to know that *one condition* resulted in a lot of work on his part. Usually, the *one condition* somehow begat a bunch of smaller conditions. Jake audibly inhaled before asking, "What condition?"

"You go in with me. Sorry to say, but it's still a man's world. If a woman is working, she'll treat me fairly for the most part. Depending on the age of the man, he'll ask if my husband is around because as a woman, I couldn't possibly figure out how a storage unit works." Hannah grimaced and rolled her eyes.

While he'd heard plenty from his niece, Katie, how women were sometimes treated like dimwits by men of a certain age, Jake liked to believe he didn't do that. Hadn't he thought Hannah sharp enough to rip off his friends? As compliments go, that might not be one she wanted to hear.

"I can do that. What if it's a young man as opposed to an opinionated geezer?"

"He might ignore both of us, but then again, he might be on camera, too. Many storage units are used to hide ill-gotten goods. It's always important to have a visual record of who rents what."

It was something he'd never thought about. If Lyre was caught on camera renting a unit after she vanished, it could be proof of her current existence if she hadn't been taken immediately after the rental. His heart pumped a little faster, knowing he was on a trail. "What should I do?"

Hannah had pocketed her keys and had her hand on the door handle. She pivoted to answer. "You'll be the silent, tall male presence. I'll do the talking. People expect that from couples."

Jake wasn't sure if that was true. As far as he could tell, Herman and Lola spoke about the same amount. As for Eunice, Gus gave her a run for her money. With Lance and Marcy, Lance chatted more than Marcy did. Jake chose not to share his findings because this was the only plan they had.

They entered the concrete building. Inside the square structure, block walls and the cement floor never let you forget you were in a garage. A poster with one curling corner advertised they sold moving boxes. Behind a makeshift counter sat a young man with earbud wires streaming from his ears. He initially glanced up at their entrance but dropped his gaze to whatever he held in hands.

Behind the distracted counter clerk was a series of keys, each labeled with a number beside it. More than a good dozen had empty spots. This surprised Jake. He was certain that technology had advanced enough that people would press in numbers as opposed to using keys. He'd ask the attendant, if only he would look up to acknowledge them. Surely, he didn't think anyone would come into the office for anything besides renting a unit? Jake spied a silver bell on the counter with a sign that read *for service, ring the bell*. He did, only to earn a glare from the young man who pulled out his earbuds.

"I saw you come in," he complained. Standing, he put his phone on the counter. "Let me guess. You lost your keys? At the Lighthouse, we give *you* the keys. This means we will have to replace the lock on your unit. That will be seventy-five dollars."

It sounded like a way to pick up some extra money since Jake seriously doubted, they didn't have extra keys hidden somewhere or maybe, a master key. Since an employee or owner replaced the lock when they did do it, they'd avoid the expense of a locksmith.

Hannah stepped forward with a spark of fire in her eyes. She lifted her chin and fixed her gaze on the gangly young man. Her eyes flicked to his name tag. "Sean, we did not come here to get an extra key. We came to rent a unit. I will assume your business is to rent units. Am I correct?"

"Yeah, what about it?"

Jake couldn't help smiling at the young man's snotty attitude, which he might come to regret in the next five seconds.

"I see," Hannah explained, running her fingers over the dusty counter, and inspecting them. "Did you know you're on camera all the time?"

"What?" Sean turned in circles, searching for the camera, until he spotted the red blinking light in a far corner aimed at the counter. "That's wrong. I got rights."

"Not as many as you'd think. This job looks pretty cushy to me. Obviously, you sit and wait for someone to walk in or call."

The boy eyed Hannah the way most would register a rat in the corner of their kitchen. At least it signaled the beginning of intelligence. Sean's bottom lips pushed out as he muttered, "It doesn't pay crap. Mr. Barclay is really cheap."

"Most unskilled jobs don't pay well and they actually expect you to do something besides sit and stare at your phone. Mr. Barclay, who happens to be a friend of mine, assured me I could get the storage unit here that I wanted."

"Yeah, there's plenty." Sean pointed at the camera. "Does it record sound, too?"

The sudden concern about someone reviewing the feed, possibly at a remote location, delighted Jake. A crime might have someone examining the past footage for hints, but the boss probably didn't care if Sean listened to music or played video games while manning the counter. No reason for Sean to know that, though.

Hannah gave him a long, measured look, and then smiled a deliciously wicked smile—possibly the same type the malevolent characters in fairy tales flashed before listing what torture they had planned for the gullible main character. "I heard someone got arrested just from watching a security tape. The unlucky perp confessed while being recorded. That was enough for a warrant."

Sean audibly gulped and asked, "What size unit do you want?"

"I'd like to be close to my friend. She has a unit at 4106. Can you get me something close?" Hannah's voice took on a wheedling tone as Sean typed on the computer. He murmured to himself. "That unit hasn't been opened for months." He glanced up to address Hannah, "I doubt you'll see your friend here."

"No matter," Hannah assured him with a smile. "I still want the closest one."

Sean grunted in response, consulted the monitor, and then pivoted, swiping a key from the backboard. "Check it out. If it's what you want, come by and I'll have you sign a contract." He consulted a card taped to the counter and read it aloud slowly. "Most of the units are 10 by 10s with a couple being 10 by 15, which is big enough for a standard car. The smaller units are fifty-five dollars a month, with the bigger ones being ninety. The first month is free with a twelve-month lease." He handed the key to Hannah without any instructions on how to reach the unit.

A chimpanzee could do as good a job as Sean, except for the talking part. As for Jake being an intimidating male presence, a derisive snort fought its way out of his throat. The boy wouldn't be able to pick him out of a line-up. Not sure what it was with some youngsters unwilling to make eye contact with senior citizens. Before the two of them could exit the front door, Sean had plugged his ears and returned to his phone.

A person could rob the place for all the attention Sean paid.

Already, the boy had forgotten his fear of being filmed. The real question was—had someone already robbed the unit in question? Only one way to find out and he hoped his Swiss Army knife was up to the task.

Chapter Twenty-Three

RUSTLING ACCOMPANIED HANNAH'S purse search. Every now and then, she pulled something out, such as her phone or hairspray and placed it next to the gear shift between the car seats. Her behavior puzzled Jake, who assumed they were going to drive to the storage unit while getting a gander at Lyre's possible rental. He doubted there would be a convenient window to peer through like a regular garage. "What are you looking for?"

"Silly string. I used to have some. In a pinch, we can use hair spray." She placed a slim leather pouch on top of her other finds and sighed. "Well, at least I have *this.*"

It appeared to be about the shape of a deluxe manicure kit. "This is not the time to be doing your nails."

Hannah snorted. "Shows what you know. It's a lock-picking kit."

Maybe he was too quick to dismiss the female of being capable of any felonious activities. "Were you planning to break *into* Greener Pastures? They pretty much let anyone in as long as you promise to pay every month."

"Ha ha! Very funny." She stuck out her tongue. "Before you go thinking the worst of me, as I imagine you already are, allow me to explain. As I mentioned, I write mysteries. In some of them, my heroine picks a lock or two, which meant I needed to learn how to do it."

That sounded reasonable. So far, the Swiss Army knife had served him well, but maybe a lock-pick kit would be an asset, too. "Did you pick up your kit when you ran out for groceries?"

"Not quite. I ordered mine online, but they are sold at big discount stores plus home and garden centers."

Jake digested the information as he glanced back over his shoulder at the office. No sign of the lackluster counter clerk, but he assumed he was hooked back up to his phone. "We need to check out the place and get out of here before Sean comes out to inquire if we need any help."

The car rumbled to life as Hannah muttered, "Fat chance of that happening. All the same, you're right. There could be a shift change, and someone who actually works might show up. We can't have that."

After checking the rear-view mirror, Hannah reversed the car slowly, then put it into drive as she worked her way through the rental units. They cruised slowly past the units, reading the numbers until Hannah floored it, careened around the corner, throwing Jake into the door.

"Hey! What was that about?" He pushed back into an upright position. Maybe if he asked nicely, she'd let him drive. Probably not. She struck him as the type who would insist on a current driver's license.

"Security camera. Every lane has one. I sped up so the license plate can't be seen. If I had thought about it, I'd have obscured it with mud or something similar."

She's not a criminal, he reminded himself. Marcy would know. Hopefully this wasn't another elaborate gag the group had decided to pull on him. They'd finally reach the unit, open it up, and there would be everyone, including Bear and Domino, shouting *Gotcha!* or something else equally irritating. "Why does the license plate matter?"

The car slowed to a crawl, allowing easy reading of numbers placed near the metal roll-down doors. "I'm not sure it *does* matter." She pointed with her index finger at the nearest unit. "Numbers are going up. We're going in the right direction."

Jake cleared his throat, aware her reply had failed to answer his query. He'd have to frame his question in another manner. "I asked…"

The car came to a stop. Hannah turned in her seat and pointed behind them. "My potential unit is back there, as is your unit in question."

"Why didn't we stop by the units?" Never mind the fact they'd have to tote boxes the extra distance. With his luck, they'd all be full of books.

"You'll see." Hannah grabbed her lock-pick kit and hairspray. "Stay behind me—we don't want you on camera. Since I'm all out of silly string, we will have to use hairspray, which will only make the lens blurry until it dries. We need a disguise and I got just the thing in the back. I got a couple of hats with mullets we can wear that we can drop off at the thrift shop later."

Mullets? Who was this woman? She must be a big fan of 90s country music or some community theater volunteer in charge of costumes. Hannah swung the door open, slipped out, and moved to open the hatchback. She grunted as she rooted through the boxes until she pulled a bright blue ball cap with flowing golden locks attached to it. "Found one. The other has to be close by."

Jake insisted on wearing the red hat with the dark mullet, convinced it gave off a masculine air as opposed to the blonde one. Hannah led the way and sprayed the camera. Her action cheered Jake a tad because he didn't want this recorded. Hannah's potential unit unlocked easily with the key, which was a plus. The empty unit smelled like cement and old paper despite it being empty. Since they were alone and inside the unit, Jake felt it was a good time to ask. "Why the cloak and dagger stuff?"

"Lola mentioned there might be mob involvement in Lyre's disappearance."

Jake blinked. No one had even mentioned they'd told Hannah about the case. "Did you deduce this from all the cases they saw on television and then asked your opinion about?"

"A little. The part where Lola told me the mob was involved this morning kinda cinched it."

He could see how that might do it. "We don't know that they *are* involved. The possibility being thrown around may just be there to distract us. I have a feeling someone much closer is involved."

"That, too." Hannah nodded her head. "Gus thought you were being followed after you visited Lyre's sister."

Gus talked to her, too! "As for that, the driver thought it was her ex-boyfriend, who sometimes harasses her."

"What if it wasn't?"

The woman had a point, and if she was right, it wouldn't be the first time the sleuths had been followed. Everyone blabbing the case details without consulting him had really honked him off. "Is there anyone you *haven't* talked to about the case?"

"You. I had a feeling you probably know more than anyone

else."

At least she had that right. Still, the loose lips and failure to mention any of this irked him. This was *his* case. If anyone chose to invite Hannah in, it should be him. "Okay, let's drop a few boxes in here."

Hannah did a doubletake. "Didn't you hear me say I was taking that stuff to the thrift store?"

"I did." For once the woman hadn't outthought him with her various mystery writer props. The thought birthed a wide smile. "I doubt we'll get what we came for on our first try. We need to establish a reason to visit. That's why we drop off the boxes. You can bring in the stuff you want to store later. I imagine people are moving stuff in and out of their units all the time."

Instead of Hannah being peeved she hadn't thought of this, she gave him a hearty slap on the back. "Good plan! Marcy mentioned you were a deep thinker."

His grin grew bigger. Who didn't like hearing something good about themselves? Hannah cocked her head to one side and stared out the open door. "There's only one issue."

As far as Jake could see, there wasn't any issue. "What?"

"If I take this unit and sign a contract, if bad guys are involved, which we both have reason to suspect they are, it could be traced back to my house."

Another good point. He'd have to do his homework to get the jump on Hannah. At least she'd be working with him as opposed to working against him. "Put down a different address. Why does it matter since you will pay online or in person?"

At one time, when Jake pretended to open an account to follow a suspect, he discovered making up an address didn't work. Thanks to the Internet, it checked the validity of everything. "It has to be a real address since they can easily check that."

"Good to know," Hannah informed him in an amiable tone. A couple of long steps brought her to the rental door exit where she turned and smirked in his direction. "Let's go get those boxes."

At the car, Jake swung his head, trying to get his extra hair to flop back in place. How men managed with long hair baffled him. Determined to be the gentleman, he picked up a box of moderate proportions and insisted Hannah stack another on top of it. With the extra box weight, Jake weaved a little but managed to remain standing. "Thunderation! What do you have in here? Rocks?"

"Just books." Hannah reached for the box. "I'll take it if it's too heavy."

Before she could put her words into action, Jake headed for the unit. No way would he let a woman carry something because he thought it was heavy. His mama raised him to be a gentleman. If he could walk on his own, then he'd carry the heavy things. When a woman was on her own, she could do whatever she wanted, even if it included moving a grand piano across a room. Hannah followed with a box of her own.

Once the boxes sat on the unit's floor, Hannah popped one open and pulled out some colorful fabric. She waved the silky swatches of fabric in the air. "Once we return to the car, we'll have to change our disguises, park on another lane, and then slip back over here on the back side to avoid being on camera as much as possible."

"The hairspray…" Jake started but remembered what Hannah had said. "I imagine it has dried already."

"Silly string would have been better. Actual criminals use spray paint," she informed him in a teacher-like tone, and then motioned to Jake that it was time to leave. He pulled the overhead door down and Hannah locked it. They casually strolled back to the car as if they had no reason to hurry, which in truth, they didn't. "Why not use spray paint?"

"Ha! It would be like putting a smoking gun in your purse."

"How so? Would people mistake you for the next great graffiti artist?"

"No one told me you were a comedian. Yes, even at my age I might be considered a vandal, even if I was only guilty of correcting the grammar on public signs. Normally, when spray paint is used on closed-circuit cameras, it's for robberies. It would be odd to walk around with spray paint in my purse. Hairspray makes sense and dries clear. Silly string makes me look like an indulgent grandma and often mimics a bird's visit. It usually falls off after a while, too."

One finger went up on Hannah's hand, "Another point would be the person who actually watches the camera monitors. He or she would know when one went dark. Usually, most miscreants do this at night, so it's much harder to tell when an outside camera has been altered."

"You know this how?" Even though he accepted Hannah as a former librarian who liked to write mysteries, some of her knowledge stretched believability.

She shot him a bemused look. "From the time ten other guys and I decided to knock over three Vegas casinos."

For the tiniest second, he speculated what role she played. His nose crinkled when he realized how readily he accepted the retired librarian as a possible criminal. If nothing else, her quick wit would energize Greener Pastures. "Oh, I get it. The movie. I'm not sure if they used spray paint on the cameras."

"Probably not. Too many people in the casino." Hannah opened the driver's door, shimmied in behind the wheel, and threw the fabric at Jake as he entered from the passenger side. He caught the filmy cloth, pleased at his quick reaction, and examined it. "These are scarves. How are they going to be a disguise?"

"Surely you've seen women wear scarves around their heads to protect their hair?"

Memories of his mother tying a scarf over her hair as protection resurfaced. Even his mother had grumbled it wasn't the best look. "There better be something in that unit that's worth all this trouble."

"Don't think of it as trouble. Think of it as fun. What else did you have lined up today?" Hannah quipped and started the car. They zipped over two lanes, parked, discarded their mullets, and Hannah tied on her scarf in a jiffy. Jake didn't fare as well. It could be his fingers refused to cooperate, somehow knowing the results.

"Let me do it." Hannah leaned toward Jake, smoothed the scarf over his hair, and tied it tightly under his chin. "Your features are too large and masculine for a woman. Try to keep your head down so no one gets a good gander at you."

"Trust me. I don't want anyone to get a good look at me wearing a scarf. Gus and Herman would laugh themselves silly. I got my pocketknife if we need a peek inside. Of course, the unit could belong to someone else. What if there is some type of alarm when the door is opened?"

With all the technology that existed, almost everything was wired for security. On the flip side, since so many alarms were always blaring, people tended to ignore them.

"I'm sure the stellar employee isn't listening for alarms with his earbuds plugged into whatever he's watching. Besides, did you notice an alarm on my unit?"

The unit they'd just exited sported concrete walls, a cement floor, a roof with some vents, and a roll down door with a key lock. There was nothing on the advertising trumpeting climate control because there was none. "Basic unit at best. No thrills."

"Exactly." Hannah moved her head down in assent, then sniffed. "I checked out the rental places. Some are ridiculously expensive, but they had all the bells and whistles. All I need is a good roof, floor, four sides, and a lock. "Don't plan on using it forever."

A turn of his wrist allowed Jake to check his watch. Almost three. It was hard to know when Sean's shift might end. "We need to get a move on. Tonight is lasagna night. Besides, we don't know how long Sean works."

Rather than arguing the point, Hannah pantomimed zipping her lips, pointed to a narrow passage between two units, and held her hand up, gesturing forward as in leading a special forces contingent behind enemy lines. It made Jake hesitate for a second, pondering if his companion had a very active imagination, watched too many movies, or possibly lived in an alternate reality of her design.

The two of them slid between the narrow openings that occurred between the units. One required turning sideways. Finally, they made it back to the unit in question, only seeing one truck with a camper on it. A heavyset man attired in a T-shirt that announced guns as his security system of choice unloaded multiple televisions. The television guy stared at them intently, then looked away, possibly not wanting to be remembered as the individual with lots of unboxed merchandise.

At 4106, Jake slid out his Swiss Army knife, selecting the tiny knife tool, and pushed it into the lock before Hannah could whip out her lock-picking tool. There were some things he could do, and he didn't need to write mystery books to know how to do it. His cheek rested against the cold metal door, listening for the telltale click. The blade stuck, sending back a tremor to his hand. "It won't move."

"Try pulling up on the handle and turning it. Works on my garage at home."

Following another's advice irked him. Jake did it because he didn't have anything better to offer. Surprisingly, the lock gave a little. Jiggling the knife along with pushing on the lock finally caused the tumblers to move in the right direction. Withdrawing his knife, he pulled open the unit door.

Inside were a few cardboard boxes and a small file cabinet. The file cabinet might tell him if this was Lyre's unit or just a wild goose chase that might get the two of them into hot water. They needed to get in and out quickly. The open door could be spotted by anyone driving by. "Would you possibly have a flashlight?"

Hannah inserted her hand into her purse and withdrew a brightly colored cylinder. "It's my super bright light. I never go anywhere without it. You need it why?"

"It might be better to do our snooping with the door closed so as not to attract attention." Proud that he'd thought of the obvious first, Jake attempted to suppress a grin. He waited until the flashlight glowed before taking off his shoe and putting it under the door to keep it from closing entirely. "Not sure if the door locks when it closes. We'd have a hard time explaining why we were stuck inside. If it comes to that, confused old person usually works. Gus is a master, but Eunice is a fair hand at it, too."

"I can imagine," Hannah commented.

The door groaned as it went down, darkening the place. The bright beam of the flashlight illuminated Jake's face. "Not on me! Point it at the file cabinet."

Jake made his way to the highlighted file cabinet. A tug on the handle assured him it was locked. Out came the pocket knife and he fiddled with it until it opened. Nothing beat a Swiss Army knife in a pinch. The light played across file folders with dates, but nothing shouted *Lyre* to him. In the second drawer, he found a laptop with a parrot sticker on it that resembled the bird who took a chunk out of his finger. "I think this is hers."

A name on anything would make Jake feel less like a criminal. For all he knew he could be taking off with a little girl's laptop, but why would she hide it in a storage unit? Underneath the laptop sat a shoebox full of tiny cassette tapes, the type used in personal recorders. Interviews, written in a slanting script, identified the contents.

They'd take that, too. He felt maybe they should go through the boxes, but a sense of urgency pushed at him. "We need to leave *now*."

Unlike Eunice, or even Lola, Hannah didn't question his assertion. Instead, she pushed open the door and handed him his shoe, which he slipped on. Nearby, they could hear the rumble of a man's voice speaking on the phone. Jake often prided himself on his still sharp hearing, which meant sometimes you heard things you didn't want to. He peeked out the unit and recognized the back of the man with the suspect televisions. Fortunately, the man stood beside his truck, gazing in the other direction.

"Yeah, I think I spotted one of those old guys you had me follow.

Weird. I'd swear he had a scarf on. It could be just an ugly woman. There's plenty of those around." He chuckled. "I tried to see where he went but he vanished."

That didn't sound good. The man wasn't sure of Jake's identification, but it wouldn't hurt to move along. Even though the temptation loomed to get a good gander at the man, Jake held the laptop by his side, trying to hide it, and pulled down the door as quietly as he could. The door that had earlier groaned about opening did likewise going down. The two of them hurried through the narrow alley to get to the car. Once inside the car, Jake said, "We need to put on the mullet caps. I think I saw someone back there. Do you have any sunglasses?"

Hannah donned a pair of shades before passing Jake his cap. His scarf fluttered to the car mat after he tore it off. The dreaded mullet cap became his preferred disguise. Sitting in the car with his cap on, no one would mistake him for an ugly woman or the old guy who visited Lorelei. Not a peep came from his companion, who started the car and slowly returned to the office. Any other woman would be flustered. A few might even be threatening to call the police, despite their own involvement in breaking and entering.

After returning to her old parking space, Hannah handed her glasses to Jake. "Here. You put those on. I need to go sign my contract. Otherwise, I might get into trouble with the law. We can't have that."

Jake held the cat eye glasses with rhinestones encrusted on them. Indecision gripped him. Should he go after her? Unlike him, no one had identified Hannah. As much as he hated it, he slipped on the glasses. He must look horrible. Curious, he flipped down his visor. His own mother wouldn't know him.

A few minutes later, Hannah, sans a disguise, returned to the car and held her hands out for the glasses.

"Where's your disguise?"

Her shoulders went up in a shrug. "I didn't have one on in the first place. It would be weird to don one when I filled out the contract. Don't credit Sean with paying too much attention to detail, but you never know. Let's hope Lance and Marcy are still there when we get back."

Chapter Twenty-Four

TIRES SQUEALED AS Hannah took the corner too fast, causing Jake to wrap his fingers underneath the car seat. His previous trip to the storage place taught him to expect the unexpected. Even though Lola accused him of not knowing what women liked, he did know driving advice sat firmly in the dislike column. Most drivers, no matter what their gender, probably echoed the sentiment. Experience had him pressing his lips shut despite his inner monologue that included exclamations such as *watch out, too close,* and *slow down*!

In the end, the fault rested with him since he had commented about the unboxed television dude's comment and how it made him wary. Apparently, that translated into *drive like a bat out of hell.* Maybe he *was* overreacting. Still, the man commented on seeing him, not the other way around. The darkness and rain obscured anyone they may have glimpsed on their way back from Lorelei's house. Besides, he accepted the driver's explanation of a vengeful ex. From online stories he'd read, they were all over the place. On the reality crime shows, they were almost always the culprit. Why would someone trail two old dudes who visited Lorelei? For all they knew, he and Gus could be relatives.

The long brick wing of the center came thankfully into view. Hannah slowed, which was another plus. He would live long enough to discover if he had Lyre's computer or had stolen a parrot fancier's machine. If so, they'd have to get it back into the storage unit. "We're here."

Hannah cut her eyes in Jake's direction as she parked and switched off the ignition. "I noticed you were a little white-knuckled on the ride back."

Jake forced a laugh. "No, no, I was fine."

"Would it help if I told you I passed one of those racecar driving courses?" Hannah offered with a smirk.

Nope, not a bit. It would make him even more paranoid getting into a car with her. He exhaled audibly and shook his head. "It wouldn't."

"Okay then, we'll go with I thought about taking one and never did. Let's see if Marcy and Lance are still here."

He couldn't figure out if she was joking about taking the class or not taking the class. When in doubt, keep-your-yap-shut advice served him well. Jake exited the car, cradling the computer, but on second thought unzipped his windbreaker, put it inside, and zipped it up. He folded his arms over his suddenly flat abs to hold the laptop in place. Hannah carried the ordinary-looking shoebox under her arm. They speed walked to the porch only to encounter Marcy and Lance wielding pet carriers. Marcy pushed one on wheels rather like luggage, which may have been due to her wonky balance, which was a result of the shooting and car crash that originally landed her in the center.

"Marcy!" Jake waved his right hand while keeping his arm banded against the laptop. "Lance…" he added the other detective's name as an afterthought. Marcy had been the official head of Senior Sleuths, but Lance had helped in multiple ways.

The two continued walking with their pet escorts. The four of them met in front of the entrance sidewalk. Marcy gave them a knowing survey. "What did you do?"

The younger woman made it sound like he and Hannah had been naughty children frolicking in the mud. "I believe I have Lyre's laptop. Hannah has tapes from her personal interviews."

Lance arched his brows. "Should I ask how you knew where to find them? It wasn't like several trained officers didn't look for this exact information."

"Ah yeah, that. The parrot told me." He cleared his throat expecting an objection. "Really! We brought the evidence to you."

Jake eased the laptop out of his jacket and presented it to Lance with both hands as if offering him a gift of great value, which it was if it was Lyre's work computer. Too bad people didn't put their name on everything as if they were going away to spend a month at summer camp. "If it isn't Lyre's, we will need to put it back. It would be weird that the parrot memorized someone else's storage unit number."

"Okay." Lance overemphasized the word making it sound like it was anything but okay as he held out both hands to accept the modest laptop. "Should I ask how you got it?"

"Better not to." If they should get in trouble helping themselves to evidence, it would be best not to have Marcy or Lance linked to them. The center door swung open, stopping the conversation. The four crowded to the left to make room for the departing couple. An awkward silence hung over them until the couple reached the parking lot.

Lance angled his head to the parking lot. "Why don't you two walk with us? It will be hard for us to juggle evidence and bring Domino and Bear with us at the same time."

The pet carrier sat on the ground with a furry head pushed against the open front crate. Jake knew without being told that he'd carry the dog. He lifted the light cage and fell in step with Lance. "What will you do next?"

"I guess I'll log the computer into evidence and have the forensics IT team look at it."

"Ah…" Jake stalled, trying to figure the most diplomatic way to say what he needed to say. "Can't you look at it on your own?"

"It's bound to be password protected and could be encrypted." Lance shrugged his shoulders. "I'm not exactly hacker material. Why do you ask?"

"Okay, you're not going to like this, but I suspect someone high up is involved in Lyre's disappearance. If you remember, she was offered police protection, which she refused before she vanished. It could be she knew some higher up in the department was guilty, which meant police protection would serve *him* rather than *her*. There are so many inconsistencies such as the headless body not being identified but assumed to be Lyre.

"The sister, who could have easily identified the corpse, headless or not, didn't do so. Peculiar, right?" Jake prompted, hoping the detectives would pick up on what he noticed and not think he was just a curmudgeon full of conspiracy theories.

"Yeah, there wasn't a definite ID. You can't make people ID someone. You'd think she'd want closure. No one pressed the woman to do so. Not sure if they brought anyone else to do so. As far as I could remember from office gossip, Lyre tended to be a bit of a loner. As you can tell, there were almost no useful notes, which was peculiar." Lance inhaled deeply. "I don't know what to think.

There's a definite chain of evidence protocol. I can't go off on my own like some cowboy."

The wheels on the pet carrier squeaked as Marcy moved closer. "I've been out of the office for a few months, but I couldn't help noticing when I came back things felt different. There's a secretive air about the place. Chief Mitchell fought against my returning, which sent up a red flag. After all, I was one of the best detectives around with a high conviction rate. You'd think he'd want me in the office."

Lance agreed, but added, "Could be you'd see too much. Put too many of the puzzle pieces together. It could be the chief isn't guilty, but is protecting some big wig who is."

"Guilty by association," Hannah pointed out. She handed the shoebox to Marcy, who had stopped by their car. "I think you need someone who's a decent hacker to find out what's on the computer, make copies, and then hand it over to evidence. Of course, all fingerprints would be wiped."

Lance's eyes sought out Marcy's. She gave the tiniest nod before Lance asked, "You know someone?"

Hannah lifted her head and pushed her shoulders back. "My nephew, Elvin. Technically, he's not my blood relative, but I've known him ever since he was in junior high. He's a premier hacker and helps in criminal cases. Corporations pay him the big bucks to see if he can break into their systems. He can get the job done."

The two detectives glanced at each other, holding an entire conversation in just one look. Marcy spoke first. "Let's do it, but we need to be quick. Who knows what happened to Lyre?"

During the fast information exchange, Jake suspected he'd turned invisible. He held up his free hand as if in school, testing his theory. Marcy must have noticed because she replied. "Yes, Jake? You have something to add?"

"I may have said this before, but not only do I think Lyre isn't dead, Lorelei knows she isn't, too."

"All right," Marcy gave him an encouraging smile. "Elaborate."

When they had their informal meetings, Marcy always allowed everyone to present their various concepts with the policy of you never knew who had a kernel of truth. Sometimes, they all did.

"On our Parrot Club trip, we discovered disreputable characters had been hounding Lorelei for information about her sister. Even though she claimed they were tabloid reporters, I think it's more likely they could be hired thugs or private eyes hired to find Lyre. Face it, an investigative reporter vanishing in a small city doesn't merit tabloid coverage, when their main fare is celebrity affairs and alien babies."

"Good point," Lance remarked. "Go on. Anything else?"

"Two things." Jake moved closer, hearing a car door close in the distance. "The parrot. Lorelei has had it for two years and clearly doesn't like it. She asked for it when the police cleared the apartment. She told me she felt obliged to take care of it because her sister *thinks the world of it*. Present tense."

"Could be a slip of the tongue," Marcy pointed out.

"Maybe," Jake conceded. "You're still relatively young, but I've said goodbye to plenty of friends and relatives. At first, it seems so impossible that they're gone you might speak of them in the present tense, not wanting to let them go. Then, as you try to accept that they're gone, you use the past tense to remind yourself. It's been two years. I doubt she'd be speaking in the present tense if she believed her sister dead. Certainly, she wouldn't still have that parrot."

"You've given us a great deal to think about," Marcy commented as she put down the shoebox on top of Domino's cage. Tired of being ignored, the black and white cat pushed a paw through the open wire and batted a fallen leaf on the blacktop.

She gestured to the shoebox. "I'm off today, and I have a personal recording device, which means I can listen to them and see if there's anything of merit before logging them into evidence. Of course, if they're mainly personal or irrelevant, there's no reason to log them into evidence." She pointed to Hannah.

"Call me on my cell as soon as you find out anything from your nephew or whatever he is."

"You got it." Hannah tucked the laptop under her arm and made a thumbs up signal with her free hand. "I'll call him right away. I was surprised he went into computers since he was such a movie buff. Always quoting lines from movies, which didn't make him popular with the other students or staff. I may have felt a little protective of him and provided a haven for him in the library."

Both Jake and Hannah watched the detectives pack up the animals and head out. Marcy turned, and arched a brow. "You never mentioned how you knew about the storage unit?"

"Ah," Jake hesitated, not willing to admit that the break in the case didn't come from hard work or deep thinking, but from a feathered creature.

"The parrot," Hannah offered, not having any qualms about sounding silly.

The information drew Lance's attention, too. He closed the rear passenger door and rested back against it. "Well done. Here I thought the Parrot Birthday Club would amount to nothing."

Amount to nothing? Jake's chin jutted out as he reacted to the good detective's words. "Why allow us to even visit Lorelei, then?"

"Why not?" Lance replied with a slight shrug. "The police had already done what they could. While I didn't expect a great deal from your plan, it couldn't hurt, and it wouldn't be traced back to the police. Fortunately, I was wrong since your Parrot Party Club scheme did work."

"Parrot Birthday Club," Jake felt the need to correct him.

"Whatever." Lance grinned. "It worked. That's all that matters. Now we need to get these pets home."

Marcy and Lance climbed into the car, closed the doors, and the engine turned over.

The two sleuths held up hands in parting before they turned back to the center. Hannah passed off the laptop to Jake. "You hold it. I'll call Elvin."

She pulled the phone out of her purse, scrolled through her contacts, and pushed a number before holding it up to her head. "Hey, Elvin! This is Hannah. I have a secret mission for you."

Even though Jake stood as close as he could without being obnoxious, he couldn't hear the man's reply, only Hannah's side.

"Really? How perfect. See you then."

Jake waited until Hannah pocketed her phone before asking, "What did he say?"

"He's not too far away. His job took him to Santa Claus, Indiana, which is about ninety minutes away. He'll drop by here on his way back home."

"That's great." Things were falling into place, thanks to Hannah. "What should I do with the computer until he shows?"

Instead of replying, Hannah turned toward the center and started strolling. With Jake's longer legs, he caught up in no time. He cleared his throat. "Ahem!"

"I'm thinking," Hannah remarked. "Call me paranoid but I think you should hide it. Somewhere no one would look."

Jake considered the winding halls, the new wing, the various activities rooms, and public areas.

"I have the perfect place." When Hannah parted her lips, Jake gave an emphatic shake of his head. "I'm not telling. How else will it remain secret? Besides, Elvin will be here in no time."

Chapter Twenty-Five

A S SOON AS Hannah and Jake entered the overheated center lobby, Eunice appeared like a genie out of nowhere, talking as she approached, "Hey, there you are."

Before Jake could even say hello, Eunice had hooked her arm with Hannah's to steer her in the desired direction. "We need to polish your croquet skills."

"What about me?" Jake asked, although he had no great desire to whack a wooden ball around. At first, he thought Eunice hadn't heard him.

She called out without even turning around. "I don't have all the time in the world. Got to work with those who show the most promise."

The dig bothered Jake some, but he knew the woman well enough to know she only poked at him to get a response. To say nothing was the ultimate revenge. He chose to say nothing, standing by the door and holding the laptop, contemplating what he should do first.

Hannah cast a backward glance over her shoulder and mouthed something indecipherable. Whatever it was featured a one syllable word. Jake deciphered it as *hide* or something similar. Something she didn't want anyone else to hear. It was hard to be secretive if everybody else knew your business. He might as well hide the laptop.

Many areas in the center remained busy, such as the dining room and the bingo lounge. No one ever went where he planned to tuck the computer. Before heading out, he surveyed the lobby, making sure he wasn't the focus of anyone's attention. A couple of ladies sat near a window peeking out, and the receptionist still had her eyes glued to her phone. It made him wonder if she had moved the entire time he was gone.

Time for him to disappear with the laptop. Jake headed out on soft feet to slip by residents without being drawn into conversations. He happened on his end location by accident when the activity director asked for his help, which resulted in his moving several boxes of donated books. Unfortunately, most donated books tended to be books so old they were falling apart, encyclopedia sets as old as the residents, and esoteric books such as the history of plastic storage ware. No one was hankering to read those. A few that might have piqued his interest had an impossibly tiny font that would require a magnifying glass to read.

It made him wonder why they even stored it. For his purposes, the small room where everything rejected went would do the trick. No reason for anyone to enter the room unless they were loading it up with more forgettable reads. Footsteps had him lunging for the room in question and pulling the door closed behind him.

Darkness enveloped Jake, but he didn't dare turn on the light and attract attention. His nose quivered as he inhaled, sucking in dust and the smell of faded paper, mustiness, and age. Voices raised in conversation faded as they went by the room. Before he flicked on the light, an uncomfortable feeling slid over his shoulders and wrapped around his neck, making it hard to breathe. What if he wasn't in the closet alone?

Foolishness. He stomped his foot to shake off the idea. There was no reason for anyone to be hanging out in the closet with the lights off. He blinked in the darkness as if that would somehow improve his focus. It didn't. Thank goodness the area probably stretched six feet at the most, allowing his fingers to graze the wall until he reached the light switch. The bright illumination made him wince after his time spent in the dark.

Jake slowly pivoted all the way around, making sure no beings of any type were hidden by the various boxes. No one—except possibly a spider or two, which he could accept. At most, it would only be an hour or so before Elvin arrived to take charge of the laptop. Caution had served him well in the past. No reason not to be careful even though everything was bumping along just fine. Someplace low would be best just in case someone decided to go through the books or by a crazy chance, start tossing them. It would take a while to work their way through the boxes.

Using the wall as a support, he knelt slowly in from of the metal shelving unit. On the bottom shelf, untidy stacks of textbooks listed to various sides. Often one stack leaned into the other, holding each other up. Jake carefully moved the books to create an interior space for the computer. Unsure what type of stress the laptop could endure, he removed his jacket to use as padding. Carefully, he built a wall of Modern Chemistry, Algebra for the New Age, and New Earth Science books that had to be circa 1940s. Not sure why anyone thought the residents would want textbooks. Did they think someone might crack open a chemistry book and read it aloud for old time's sake?

His book wall stood straight, which momentarily pleased him until he realized its evenness drew attention to it. Jake knocked down a couple of books on top of his wall and left them lying. Now *that* resembled the rest of the room. Standing with a bit of groaning since no one else was around, Jake dusted his hands and contemplated his next actions. He might as well go to the courtyard since the other sleuths would be there perfecting their game.

Laughter sounded as Jake exited the door. Two of the female residents passed by, giggling, and whispering. A quick check of his clothes assured him everything was as it should be. It could be a smear of dirt on his face due to the storage room not receiving cleaning of any kind. He ducked into the hall restroom but saw nothing out of the ordinary that would cause a chuckle. Sure, his nose stretched out to the right a centimeter more than he'd like, but it had always been that way. Or it had been after he got into a fight with a drunk sailor while protecting a USO entertainer.

Oh well. He shrugged his shoulders and turned to leave, only to hear more merriment as he stepped out. What was going on?

"Oh my," said one of the male residents named Chester, wheezing the words between chuckles. He jabbed one finger up the hall. "Did you see what I saw?"

"No," Jake replied, rather wishing he had. It was like not knowing the punchline of a joke everyone else knew.

Chester wiped away a tear. "Maybe you can catch up with them. It reminded me of Uncle Miltie. Two dudes in dresses asking for Hannah Holt. No one by that name lives here. They claim to be old neighbors of hers." His brow puckered. "Why are those guys here? Now that I think about it, despite the floral dresses and lipstick, they seemed like rough characters."

Jake leapt into action, rushing down the hallway. After ten yards or so, his rush of adrenaline left him gasping in front of the courtyard windows. On the other side of the glass, a leisurely scene played out with the senior sleuths tapping colored balls with wooden mallets.

What in the world could the woman have done to have two rough characters after her? Could they be victims of her astronaut wife con? His hand went back to rub his neck. Maybe they weren't as easy going and understanding as he was. Nothing much happened at the center until Hannah arrived.

Maybe it wasn't Hannah, but something she did. Acting on his assumption, he pushed open the door and strolled over to Hannah. The woman held her croquet mallet loosely and waved with her free hand. Nearby, Herman lounged on a bench with his eyes closed.

"Come to finally practice?" Hannah held out the mallet to him.

"Uh," he hesitated but accepted the offered mallet with his fingers wrapping around the stick tightly. "Out of curiosity, what address did you put on your storage unit form?"

"Ah, that." Her shoulders went up in a shrug. "Couldn't think of anything. I did have a card from the center, so I used that. Why?"

His initial suspicion started morphing into something closer to reality. "Did you put your name as Hannah Holt?"

"Of course, I did. It *is* my name." One brow arched a little higher than the other. "Is this leading somewhere?"

Herman opened his eyes. "Yeah, I'd like to know, too."

"Apparently, there are two guys in Greener Pastures dressed as women and doing a poor job of it from what I hear. They're asking for Hannah Holt. It's fortunate no one knows you. So far, the guys are probably running in circles with the information the residents are feeding them."

Herman cleared his throat. "I wouldn't count on that. Eunice is extolling Hannah as her secret weapon. I'm betting more than a few people will remember her name."

Not what he wanted to hear. A small groan escaped him. "It may be worse. I think it might be someone after Gus and me. It could be something to do with the case."

"Oh no!" Hannah pressed a hand against her chest. "We need to hide."

The courtyard boasted benches and a few oversized pots with faded flowers but nothing sizable. Hannah had taken a step in one direction, but finding nothing workable, she stepped backward and turned slowly. "I'm not sure where we can go."

Herman pushed up from the bench. "I know where we can go. The bingo lounge. Everyone thinks old people look alike. It's the perfect place. Today is candy bar bingo and that means a big crowd. I'll go get the girls ready."

Getting them ready might be bringing his wife's walker closer to her, but Eunice would be the real issue. Hell or high water wouldn't get her moving unless she wanted to and, bathed in a competitive spirit with the croquet tournament happening soon, she wouldn't want to leave for anything.

Maybe Gus would have better luck. Jake swung his head side to side looking for his friend. "Where's Gus?"

"Little boy's room," Herman answered as he opened Lola's walker.

Not good, not good at all. He had no clue what thugs expected to extract from himself or Gus. If they were after the laptop, why didn't they break into the storage unit to begin with? His attention switched from watching the glass doors, hoping to see Gus wandering back to Herman, who wasn't having much luck rounding up the women.

Lola flourished her phone. "I'm calling Marcy."

"You can do that from the bingo room," Jake fired back.

"No, I can't. It's too noisy." Lola held up a finger and put the phone up to her ear.

At least Marcy would know they were in trouble, but not soon enough to prevent any broken bones. His gaze lingered on Hannah, who riffled through her purse, and then moved on to Eunice, who picked up the wooden balls spread across the lawn and deposited them into a pile. "We're not getting ready for a snowball fight."

The wiry woman held up a ball menacingly. "You know my aim is true. These will hurt a lot more than a snowball. The downside is they don't have much range."

No one was listening to him when he was trying to keep them safe. Herman, maybe, but the women were not. His hand went back to rub his stiff neck as his eyes searched for Gus, peering into the center through the windows that surrounded the courtyard. No sign of Gus's bald pate, but he did see burly figures in floral dresses and cheap wigs coming down the hall.

"There they are!" Jake yelled, then regretted it as the figures stopped and turned in their direction and pointed at him. Oh great. He just happened to be the one guy who didn't look like every other old man. Darn his luxurious dyed hair. His grip tightened on the mallet, hoping it would be up to the job. Behind him, Hannah yelled, "I found it!"

She pushed a pink handgrip device at him. "It's a stun gun. They must be close enough for you to touch them with the stun gun. Let me arm it."

The device made an electronic humming sound that made Jake wary, but he carefully took it from Hannah as the doors opened. Hannah whispered. "We got this. I got my mace too so stay out of my spraying range."

If he learned nothing else from being in the Sleuths, it was trying to talk your way out of a situation first since brawn wasn't on their side. "Can I help you, gentlemen?"

The heavyset one stabbed a finger in Jake's direction. "He's the one. Let's take him with us."

So far, the soft answer approach wasn't working, and Jake's blood pressure must be spiking. He could feel his heart running as if he were in the Kentucky Derby. He checked to see Hannah's location and moved in front of her. "You must have me mistaken for someone else."

It could be time to switch to the confused elderly guy routine, but before he could, the larger guy lunged for him. Jake stumbled back, swinging his mallet awkwardly with his left hand, and then he remembered the stun gun in his right hand. As the man approached, he cowered as if afraid, hiding his right hand by his side. Using the fluorescent stun gun, he made contact where the dress gaped, exposing a hairy belly.

"Ugh!" the man yelped before dropping to the ground, twitching, and cursing at the same time.

A shrill voice, which Jake identified as Eunice's, screamed, "Attack!"

The slender cohort became the target of wooden balls and a few well-placed croquet mallet swings. At first, the man held his hands up to protect his face from the initial assault. He dropped them and reached behind and swore. Without thinking out the situation the way any normal person would, Jake shifted into reaction mode and took two running steps and launched himself at the man before he could rip open his dress to extract his gun.

The incapacitated thug lying on the ground kept groaning but managed a hoarse shout, "Shoot him!" which confirmed Jake's theory about the gun. While the tackle brought the leaner man down, it didn't stop him from rolling or bucking to try to loosen the hold. "Get off me, you crazy old coot!"

Jake held on, even though his muscles shouted at him to let go. He gritted his teeth, determined to keep the man from getting to his gun. From a distance, he heard, "I got this!"

A long dust mop hit him in the face, making it hard to breathe and see.

"Oops!"

Jake recognized Gus's voice. More than once had he heard that exclamation right after something awkward happened. Still, he held on despite not being able to see and his muscles aching.

"Roll, Jake, roll! Now!"

He heard the urgency in Hannah's words and responded to them, releasing the perp, and trying to roll but not getting very far since the adrenalin surge died about the same time. A hiss and a heavy cloud of mist settled on the ground, touching Jake, and making his eyes sting and breathing problematic.

Cursing sounded nearby interspersed with a litany against the elderly. Hannah's voice came closer. "Oh, Jake. I'm so sorry. I told you to roll."

All he could do was lie there and try not to moan. His hand went up to touch his eyes, but another hand took his. "Don't rub it. Just makes it worse."

His hand dropped as he concentrated on his breathing which hurt, too. He thought he heard Eunice. "You called the police, didn't you?"

Gus answered. "I did."

More voices erupted around him. Shuffling feet along with running feet entered the courtyard, making him wince, afraid someone might step on him. A brief whine of a police siren added to the cacophony. If only he could see, breathe easy, and stand up. He could be more of a help than an obstacle.

"What happened to Jake?" a voice he recognized as Marcy's asked.

"I, um..." Hannah started, then hesitated. "...accidentally sprayed him with Mace."

Lola leaned over Jake—he recognized her strong perfume. "Herman went to get some milk. Since it's almost supper time, he could grab some off a tray or the wing fridge. Here he is."

"Wait!" Marcy spoke right before a wave of icy cold milk hit his face, relieving some of the burning. "I was going to say dish soap mixed with water works better. The paramedics are on their way."

A milky, battered Jake pushed up into a sitting position. "I'm okay outside of a few bruises. I want to know what's going on with the thugs, drag show and all."

Marcy patted his shoulder. "Good thing we weren't too far away. Domino slipped out of his carrier and we had to stop the car to recapture him. He's quite the escape artist."

That pulled a chuckle from the surrounding sleuths. Uniformed police, who had arrived with Marcy and Lance, escorted the handcuffed thugs out, pushing through the crowd of curious bystanders.

At the edge of the group stood a thin young bespectacled man wearing a black T-shirt. Jake blinked, trying to bring the man into better focus. No, he didn't know him. As he came closer, he could read his T-shirt, which said *The Truth is in The Hard Drive.* That must be Elvin.

"Aunt Hannah, what's going on?"

Chapter Twenty-Six

ELVIN RUSHED OVER to Hannah's side and placed an arm around his aunt. "Are you okay?"

"Oh yes," she exclaimed in a breathy voice, patting her nephew's arm. "This is the most excitement I've had in forever. You were right about my being around other people. It's much more fun than being home alone."

"This isn't what I expected." He gave the sleuths a suspicious look and raised one eyebrow. "I expected a senior citizen to be more low keyed."

Paramedics entered the courtyard, and Marcy directed them to Jake first. He suffered their checking his heart rate and blood pressure but wished they wouldn't chatter so much. It was hard to decipher what everyone else was saying with the medic questioning him. Even though the medics urged him to go to the hospital for more thorough testing, Jake refused. The possible final chapter to the cold case could happen while he sat around in a drafty robe waiting for an X-ray that would prove nothing.

"I'm good. If I feel like I'm not, I'll notify the nurse."

The medic nodded his head, and then went over to examine the other sleuths and received similar brush-offs. He signaled his partner and announced to the group, "Okay, we're out of here. Since you're already in a facility which provides medical care, I'm sure an extra vigilant eye will be kept on you six. Try to hold down the wild parties."

They all chuckled and waved at the departing medics. Lance squatted beside Jake to help him to his feet. He'd like to tell the younger man he could do it on his own, but frankly, he appreciated the help. The medic gave him some extra strength aspirin for the pain, which made him sleepy, or maybe exhaustion made him tired. Whatever it was, he wasn't going to sleep while Elvin hacked the laptop.

After a brief discussion, the Sleuths plus Elvin agreed to meet in Herman and Lola's suite since it was the largest. Marcy left to retrieve the animals and Elvin offered to assist. Before Jake could stagger back to his room and change into dry clothes, Hannah slipped over and kissed his cheek. "You're my hero."

Lance, who had been standing close by, joined Jake as they both watched Hannah leave the courtyard. "You still wary of her?"

"Not as much as I was," Jake had to admit with a rueful expression. "However, with the fairer sex, I have learned to assume nothing." Both men chuckled as they made their way to Jake's room.

After a clothing change and a computer retrieval, Lance and Jake arrived at the crowded suite. Even Bear and Domino roamed the room.

Elvin sat down at the table in front of the laptop. He wove his fingers together, and then stretched them outward as if an expert safecracker warming up for the job. The first thing he did was pop the lid open and hit the power button. "It's dead."

Obviously, it was dead. Who knew how long it had sat in the storage unit? After some spirited discussion, Jake recognized the brand was like his. "Just a minute, I think I have a power cord that might work."

Even though he'd prefer to sprint to his room, his body only allowed a firm walk at best. With the cord retrieved, they were ready to start again. Elvin plugged it in and it flickered to life. The group huddled behind him, often jostling for a prime viewing spot until Elvin cleared his throat.

"This is delicate business. I'm a maestro of hacking so please, I need space and silence."

His announcement resulted in the sleuths taking a collective step backward. Elvin pulled a device out of his pocket and stuck it into the USB port. There was some chirping, and the device lit up.

"What's that and what is it doing?" Eunice asked, leaning over Elvin's shoulder.

"It's my go-to when I don't know the computer owner. Most people usually base passwords on family, pets, birthdates, or hobbies. Their passwords aren't as clever or indecipherable as they think.

Jake made a mental note to change his computer password.

The computer dinged. "We're in," Elvin announced. "Let me check out a few things." His fingers flew over the keyboard. Black letters showed up against a white background. "Okay. This computer was activated six years ago by someone named L. Y. R. E." Elvin spoke each letter individually.

A cheer went up.

Eunice poked him. "What else does it say?"

The computer hacker glanced at Hannah, who cleared her throat. "I think it's dinner time. Why don't we all go and eat, then come back and see what Elvin has come up with. He works much better on his own."

Mild grumbling sounded, but it didn't stop the group from heading out to the dining room. After all, it *was* lasagna night. Jake hoped no one had taken over their table. Lance joined them, leaving Marcy behind to supervise Elvin and watch over the pets.

The meal was one of his favorites with a big wedge of garlic bread, tossed salad, and caramel pudding cake for dessert. Jake sped through the delicious food, anxious to get back to the room. It had to be the quietest meal the sleuths ever enjoyed. A few of the other residents occasionally gave them odd stares, possibly speculating on if they were all mad at each other or wondering about the brouhaha in the courtyard.

Lance picked up food for Elvin and Marcy. He carried it back to the room, so there was no one to ask when the right time to come back would be. The last bite of caramel pudding cake he savored. It might be his favorite dessert, but it didn't show up in the meal rotation that much. Might as well appreciate it when he could. As he put his fork down, he could feel all eyes on him. The other sleuths must have eaten much faster. Eunice asked, "Can we go back yet?"

She asked him as opposed to doing exactly what she wanted to do. It must be her way to acknowledge him as the leader of this case. It felt good. Call him conceited, proud, or whatever, but he enjoyed it. He waited a full minute. "I think if we proceed down the hall at a leisurely pace, it should be fine."

The sleuths bolted from the table with Gus and Eunice in the lead. Jake pushed his chair in and joined Lola and Hannah who said, "I hope Elvin has hacked whatever he needs to hack since he prefers to work alone."

"Me, too," Jake agreed. "One thing I can assure you about

Greener Pastures is *you'll* never be alone."

"That's a good thing," Hannah assured him. "I'm seeing the benefits of regular social interaction."

"Um, what happened in the courtyard wasn't regular." He didn't want Hannah to get the wrong idea and think living at the center resembled a dive bar where fighting could break out at any time.

Lola chuckled. "We only have moments of extreme peril every couple of months." She elbowed Hannah. "If your heart can take it."

"It can." Hannah cut her eyes to each one of them. "Maybe we could have more frequent moments of peril."

"Depends on the case and how fast we solve it. Some, I imagine, involve no car chases, no thugs, or any type of danger," Jake added to see how Hannah might react. Her brows furrowed together as she considered the possibility.

"How many of those have you had?"

Disappointment colored her tone. All cold cases needed to be solved, but those involving simple research on the Internet were probably about as interesting as reading one of the textbooks in storage.

"So far, we've had none," Jake told her and then asked, "Did you get your stun gun back?" In the hubbub, he never even considered it.

"Yep. I picked it up before we left. Marcy's the one who advised me to get a stun gun, being a woman on my own. I need to keep track of it. Not sure if the staff would confiscate it."

"Not sure, either." Jake gave his head a slow shake. "It did come in handy, though. Thanks for sharing."

"You're welcome to use it in the future. I'm not quite sure if *I* could ever use it on a person."

The conversation stopped as they reached their destination. Outside the door, the sound of a printer penetrated.

They pushed open the door slowly. Lance and Marcy were hovering over the laptop while Elvin chowed down on the lasagna. Gus, Herman, and Eunice crept closer, but were waved off by Marcy. "Back up guys. This needs to be hush-hush. You're right, Jake. Some of the local big wigs included the chief of police and the mayor, which explains the cover-up and why Lyre took off."

Lance gestured to the computer. "Lyre kept a journal where she detailed all her activities. If you're wondering why no one knew about the rental unit, she rented it in her parrot's name, Parody. She even mentions going into hiding. The question is where did she go and when will she return?"

Good question. Jake nodded his head in agreement. At last, things were starting to fit together. No thanks, though, to certain folks who made sure there was very little to follow up on the cold case. If it wasn't for the Senior Sleuths' tenacity and unlimited free time, the case might have never been solved.

Epilogue

THE CROQUET TOURNAMENT came on a clear day with an occasional errant breeze, which shook brightly colored leaves from their trees, showering the modest crowd below. The crisp air had senior citizens bundling up in sweaters, mufflers, and a few sported fingerless gloves like those hobos used to wear in vintage movies. A burst of static sounded as the activity director tapped the microphone.

Marcy and Lance had arrived earlier to give them the low down on the investigations and arrests. "Things are proceeding as they should. The laptop and its contents served as a big drift net to catch all the slimy characters."

"Oh!" Marcy interrupted, "We went back to the storage unit and found all sorts of incriminating evidence in the file cabinet. Pictures of funny bookkeeping, checks written to known criminals for jobs done, even copies of emails. I have no clue how Lyre got this stuff, but it's dynamite. No wonder criminal types feared her."

Despite the conclusion being forgone, Jake still worried about the reporter. "Have you seen Lyre?"

"No." Both detectives answered in unison. Marcy raised a brow and spoke. "We went by to talk to Lorelei and noticed the parrot had vanished. Lorelei told us her sister decided to start over in a new location. She felt there would be hard feelings here."

"Understandable." Most criminals rationalized their behavior and often their families and friends did the same. "Did she say anything else?"

Lance rolled his eyes upward as if trying to remember and then smiled. "Lyre mentioned she deliberately talked to the parrot, saying the storage unit number, figuring someone would recognize it for what it was. No one did until you."

No teacher ever bragged on his scholarly knowledge, but it pleased him that he could still figure out things. "I can't take all the credit. Hannah's mentioning of the Lighthouse Rental is what sparked it for me. Whatever happened to those thugs?"

"Oh yeah, them. I appreciate you all swearing out assault and battery charges. Those two turned on each other to get a better deal. They also implicated Sean, the do-nothing counter clerk who was letting them use unrented units to hide their stolen goods. It turns out they weren't associated with the cold case at all. They were afraid you saw them ripping off houses in Lorelei's neighborhood. Once you were spotted again, Gordy, the bigger dude, was sure you were spying on him. Apparently, he had double-crossed another thief and was certain you were reporting back to him."

"An old guy. He was afraid of an old guy?"

Lance shrugged his shoulders. "Go ahead and laugh, but older folks are moving into crime more and more because people never suspect them."

Lance had a point. Not so long ago, Jake read about a drug courier being an elderly woman in a fast-food uniform. Whenever anyone saw her, they assumed she was getting off from work as opposed to carrying huge amounts of cash in her backpack.

Gus waved his hand. "Excuse me. Was it Gordy and Company

chasing us the night we visited Lorelei?"

"Yep." Marcy pressed her lips together as if something amused her. "They did, but not for the reason you might think. First, they saw you lurking around the area they had just robbed, which they found suspicious. Then you were picked up by Gordy's old girl-friend. It's unclear if he was following you or harassing the ex. In the end, she lost them anyway."

"Wow!" Gus replied, which Jake echoed. "Wow! By the way, I did give her a good tip, but on second thought, it should have been bigger."

"True. Much bigger." Lance agreed.

Lola cleared her throat before speaking. "What about the body they found? No one ever identified her."

Lance shook his head and sighed. "I did try to find out what happened to the remains. Apparently, she's ashes now. Not even sure where the ashes are. Used to be unclaimed bodies were put in a pauper's grave. Cremation was probably chosen because of the decayed condition of the body. I'm sure the chief was no fan of Lyre, aware she'd dug up information on his nefarious activities. Still, I wonder if he encouraged the belief that the body could be Lyre's. It would give the woman some breathing room and time to skedaddle. Could be he had more selfish reasons, such as being told to get rid of her. Don't know." The detective shook his head, possibly wondering if they'd ever know the identity of the woman pulled out of the river.

The sound of hand clapping broke the group out of the collective funk.

"All right team!" Eunice called out. "Case is solved. Let's gather and plan."

Team Domino huddled near the exit door, exchanging game

strategies. Since the fall weather decided not to cooperate as far as being warm, the planned black and white polka-dotted shirts had morphed into ball caps with white dots, although the women went with scarves at their necks, tied in a rakish fashion. Despite every-thing, they were all alive and moving. The guilty awaited prosecution. Best of all, Lyre was alive and reunited with her parrot, Parody.

"Can I butt in here for a minute?"

Jake's inquiry interrupted Eunice's talk about rattling the other team by acting confident and trash talking. "Sure. After all your work on the latest case, you've earned it."

Did she just say what he thought she did? His hand went up to cover his heart. "Thank you. I appreciate it. Okay, as you all know, we haven't practiced that much. Unless you count outsmarting bad guys."

His remark caused the sleuths to giggle, as he expected. The sound resulted in happiness flooding his body. Things were back to the way they used to be or maybe his perspective had changed. Before, he wanted credit for solving a cold case single-handedly, like a superhero. Even superheroes formed teams and alliances and were stronger for it. A movement in his peripheral vision had him turning to see Hannah pointing in his direction. "You're the man. You did it."

Gracious praise, but he hardly merited it. "*We* did it," he cor-rected. If it hadn't been for all the little tricks that came from your mystery research writing, we might not have solved the case so quickly or not at all. Anyhow," he held out his hands, his palms open skyward. "I'm grateful for good friends, great work, and old-fashioned fun. Croquet is a game. Let's treat it as such. It doesn't matter if we win or lose."

Eunice made an offended snort, but everyone else agreed with him. When their team name came up, they played, even chuckling at their bad shots. When members of another team tried to trash talk them, they simply nodded and agreed they were hopeless amateurs.

At the end of the day, they came in second to last. When the activity director announced the results, Eunice huffed a little, but muttered, "Thank goodness for the Little Rascal Gang. Without them, we would have been dead last."

Usually, silence greeted Eunice's pronouncements since no one was sure how to take them. Should you agree with her as to not rile her up? Not saying anything worked best, but not being part of the gang, Hannah ignored the usual protocol.

"Let's go celebrate. Who wants to go out for ice cream?"

"What are we celebrating?" Eunice inquired with arms crossed in a surly manner.

Not fazed by the attitude, Hannah just grinned. "Having fun together."

To think he wasn't a fan of Hannah becoming a Senior Sleuth. It was the best decision he never made.

The End

Available February 2021

The Wedding Cakes Blues

Chapter One

THE SWEET, RICH smell of chocolate wafted from the oversized oven, danced around the stainless-steel appliances crammed into the tidy kitchen, before slipping into the small waiting area where customers could wait patiently for their morning cup of joe and a sweet treat. Della Delacroix arched a brow and strained her ears for any jingles of the mounted bell on the entry door indicating incoming or exiting customers. Not a sound—if she discounted her mother humming show tunes. If her mother was humming, it meant no customers. Della closed her eyes and sighed.

It wasn't a bit like that movie where a guy built a ballpark and all the baseball greats of old came to play. She thought it would be enough to bake delicious cakes and pastries at reasonable prices to ensure a thriving business. Her nose wrinkled and her top lip curled at her former optimistic outlook about how easy running a bakery would be. The oven buzzer's shrill tone had her hurrying to check her chewy brownie cookies. Timing was everything. Too long and they'd be dry. She donned oven mitts, opened the oven doors, received a blast of heat, then removed the finished cookies.

Her mother, Mabel, strolled into the room, placed her hands on her ample hips, and sniffed the air appreciatively. "Yummy. Gimme a sample."

"No, you don't," Della teased. "Aren't you trying to lose weight for your dating profile pic?" She pivoted, moving the tray of fragrant sweets out of her mother's reach.

"Seriously! You act like you don't know me." She gestured to her well-proportioned figure. "Haven't you heard men prefer women with a little padding?" A chuckle punctuated her comment. "Besides," she sighed, "I think putting up a dating profile is a bit too soon for me. However," She pointed a manicured finger in Della's direction. "Not you."

Not this again. It was the twenty-first century and women could live full lives without marrying and having the usual two children. As a good daughter, Della chose not to mention she wasn't interested in dating. More accurately, she wasn't interested in anyone her mother, her friends, or distant relatives, thought were suitable for her. They never were. "Mother. It's been seven years since Dad died. He'd want you to be happy."

A snort sounded and Mabel narrowed her eyes. "If he wanted to make me happy, he would have taken better care of himself. Ate better and exercised." Mabel waited until the cookie tray went onto the counter before picking up a spatula to lift off a freshly baked cookie. She missed the irony that she just complained about her deceased husband's eating habits while reaching for a calorie-rich goodie. A rapturous expression crossed her face as she chewed. "This is good!" she declared. With her mouth still full, she reached for another cookie. "Really good."

The praise made Della smile. Compliments on her cooking were always appreciated. "Thanks, Mom. Maybe you could be my testimonial person for an ad. We have to get more people acquaint-ed with our scrumptious fudgy brownie cookies."

"So true." She gestured with a cookie. Her mother agreed, giving an emphatic nod. "There's got to be something we can do. I didn't invest your father's insurance money just to watch it go down the drain."

The words made Della cringe. No way had she intended for her cake decorating dreams to suck in her mother, too. Even though she never asked for help, Mabel insisted on forwarding her the money when the bank refused to do so. Businesses failed every day, but Della had no intention of being just another statistic.

She even came up with a cute name, Cupid's Catering Company. Maybe that was a mistake. People who wanted a simple cake, a donut, or even a fast lunch assumed a catering company didn't do basic food. A large wooden sign with the bakery name and tiny chubby cupids with rosy cheeks cavorting on it had cost her plenty. She couldn't afford to change the name on the sign or on her website now. Her energy would be better served to concentrate on the catering side.

She took the spatula from her mother and used it to carefully maneuver the chocolate cookies onto lace doilies. "At least we have the McCormick/Lawson wedding coming up."

Mabel mumbled through a full mouth, "Bridezilla." Her accom-panying eye-roll filled in the things she didn't say.

Dealing with Ellie McCormick for the last six weeks not only added to Della's stress levels but caused tension headaches, too. Ellie had changed the menu at least five times. The upside was they hadn't ordered too many supplies. Other vendors had complained about the difficulty of working with Ellie, which made her feel better. It meant it wasn't just her. This time next month the wedding would be over and she'd be getting bookings galore from wedding guests. A well-planned catering spread would serve as her audition for future brides and mothers of the bride to be.

"Remember! Two hundred of Charlotte's best people will be the guests."

Mabel snorted. "I've heard that a half dozen times. You've probably heard it more."

"True." She placed the last cookie on the doily and lifted the tray to carry into the front area. The breakfast crowd might be slow to non-existent, but their location close to the courthouse had many of the workers stopping in for a quick snack with the cookies being a favorite. "All I have to do is grin and bear it. I can handle difficult people as long as they have money in their grubby hands."

She tossed off the last words as she backed into the swinging door that separated the kitchen from the shop area. A slight clearing of a throat had her turning fast causing the cookies to slide on her tray. Fortunately, she stopped the slide by placing the tray on the counter and smiled at the handsome bearded man dressed in a pea coat that was suitable for the chilly, misty weather. "How can I help you?"

He reached into his wallet and flourished a ten-dollar bill. "I got money in my grubby hand. Hope that means I can get a black coffee and something sweet. Those cookies you almost dropped might do the trick."

"Ah, yes." Color flooded her cheeks. Not only had the man overheard her remark, he had no hesitation to tease her. Some people might call it flirting. The thought had her crinkling her nose. Men didn't flirt with Della, that much she knew. All through school, what eligible males wanted from her was her homework or the answers to an upcoming test. Once her baking skill emerged right around her junior year, her brownies were another thing in demand.

No reason to flirt back since nothing would come of it. She poured the coffee in a to-go cup without asking if he intended to stay. He struck her as someone who had places to be.

"Sweetheart, I got a plan to help jumpstart your love life!" her mother called out before pushing the door open and seeing the sole customer. "Oh, sweet pea. I had no clue you were busy."

Somehow, she doubted that. Voices carried, but she never heard the front door bell ring either. "Not too busy." She smiled at her customer as she handed him the capped cup of coffee.

Her mother plopped her elbow on the counter and rested her chin in her upturned hand. "Hello. You look interesting. Where did you come from?"

Good heavens, not this again. The younger men who Mabel chose to chat up probably thought her overfriendly overtures meant cougar city, but in truth, her mother was shopping for Della as opposed to herself, which wasn't much better. Della wrapped the cookie and stuck it into a white bakery bag. "Okay. That will be four dollars and twenty-seven cents."

Bearded and Handsome grinned as he handed over the ten-dollar bill. "Very reasonable. Hope the cookie is as delicious as it smells."

"It is." Some might call her cocky, but she knew where her skills lay and her brownie fudge cookies were the best.

"I'll vouch for that," her mother offered and brushed at her mouth to rid herself of any crumbs that might reside. "I didn't catch your name. I thought I knew everyone worth knowing in town."

Would the ground just open and swallow Della? She forced a laugh. "My mom is such a jokester."

She shot her mother a significant look hoping she'd tone down her attitude. As if expecting this, Mabel turned her head away from Della and focused on the stranger who grinned at her mother. He arched an eyebrow, transferred the cookie bag and coffee to his left hand, and stretched out his right hand toward Mabel. "I'm Ethan Stone. Pleased to meet you."

Mabel took the offered hand and gave it a hearty shake. "Pleased to meet you, Ethan. I'm Mabel Delacroix. And you already met my daughter, Della."

Ethan nodded convivially and cut his eyes to Della, then back to Mabel. She could almost hear the wheels in his head turning, wondering why anyone would name their daughter Della Delacroix. "My parents were expecting a boy. Somehow, they thought Jason wouldn't serve for a girl."

"I would agree with that."

Her mother sniffed. "You always tell that story in such a judgy way. Please remember I was still under anesthesia. It took a while before I considered that your first name sounded a bit like your last. By then, it was too late." She waved her hand to rid herself of any condemnation.

Mabel tsked. "What you must think of us. Don't let me keep you from your big important job."

He touched a finger to his temple. "I'm the one who should be blushing now. I came here to ask you questions pertinent to my case and end up buying sweets and chatting. I'm a private investigator."

"What case? What questions?" Unease unfurled in Della's stomach like one of those resurrection plants you add water to and they miraculously come to life. Her water tended to be the unknown and uncertain, which often were the same.

"Jeffrey Lawson. Have you seen him lately?" The words hung in the air changing the former light-hearted atmosphere.

As the potential groom of Bridezilla, Della had seen him squirm as Ellie complained about how provincial their sample menus were. A glazed look had settled on him when Ellie changed the menu for the fourth time. Most of the time, the well-groomed heir to Lawson Industries acted as if he'd rather be anywhere else but listening to his fiancée rage against the world and threaten financial as well as legal repercussions. "Well, I've have seen him. Maybe a week ago. He was with Ellie."

Ethan shook his head and grimaced. "Not good. You were the last wedding vendor I've contacted. I hoped you might know something the others didn't. Thanks, anyhow."

His brow furrowed as he worked out whatever issue troubling him. Both Mabel and Della held up a hand in farewell, but he never even noticed. Ethan exited, clutching his bakery bag and coffee.

Della waited until the door closed before speaking. "Now, I'm worried there might not be a wedding. The man probably hightailed it out of here after the fourth menu change."

"Could be," her mother agreed. "It's more likely his family had him kidnapped to prevent the nuptials."

Out of the two of them, Della considered herself to be the more practical one. Only this time, her mother might be right.

Even though it might be selfish on her part, she needed this wedding. After insisting the menu couldn't be changed again, Ellie McCormick had agreed to the final menu. Although, Bridezilla could still try. "There's only one thing we can do. We have to find

Jeffrey Lawson."

Her mother rested one hand on her hip and regarded her daughter with disbelief. "How are we supposed to do that? It seems to me Ethan is doing that now and he doesn't sound like he's having much luck. Why would *we* succeed when he hasn't?"

Normally, she'd be the naysayer, but she *needed* to cater this event and earn the money it provided. Della walked over to her mother and hooked arms with hers. "We make a great team in the bakery and outside of it, too. As far as tracking a missing man, you got a gossip hotline second to none that can throw light on why the man is nowhere to be found."

Her mother sniffed. "I may be good, but it doesn't take a genius to understand why Lawson is making himself scarce. He's found himself hogtied to Elsie McCormick. I'd chew my leg off to get away.

Della held up her hand. "You have a point, but it has to be more than that. Why hire an investigator? We need to find out why the man ran off? Or even whom the man ran off *to*?"

Her mother's expression morphed from doubtful to curious. "That does sound up my alley. What's your role?"

"Analytical, of course. We know why he ran—mostly. I need to figure out how to allay his fears, get him back, and save our event." Even though her words were bold, Della had no clue how it would work, but work it had to since this was her first wedding catering job.

"Count me in!" her mother chimed.

Author Notes

The Over the Hill Gang series was written after spending a decade working as a cook in a convalescent and retirement center. The characters of Lola and Gus were loosely based on two favorite former residents. The layout of the facility is based on my own retirement center. The city, New Albany, is a real place. Most of the time, the sleuths are headed out on Grant Line Road.

For those who are wondering if this is the last book in the series, the answer is no. The senior sleuths still have a lot energy and sassiness left. Keep your eyes out for the next book **Late for the Wedding** where the senior sleuths take on *two* cold cases to decide, which gender is the better crime solver.

Love to see you. In the meantime, stay in touch via my newsletter. Sign up at
www.morgankwyatt.com.

Subscribers find out about exclusive freebies, contests, and personal appearances.
If you feel like writing a review, please do.

Reading takes you to your happy place.

MK Scott
www.morgankwyatt.com

www.ingramcontent.com/pod-product-compliance
Lightning Source LLC
Chambersburg PA
CBHW051948220626
47052CB00004B/855